Always in My Heart

Conceived as a wedding gift

to Margo

Source material provided by

CJ Gorius

Published by CJ Gorius
Asheville, NC

First Printing August 2013

In the late 1950's, in a little New England town, Conrad Holbrook and Mariella Cuore were high school sweethearts. When College came, the two said a painful goodbye. They thought they would never see each other again. They were right for fifty-four years. Then, they were wrong. All it took was one phone call … everything for Conrad and Mariella changed.

Always in my Heart tells the tender story of young love deferred, only to be rediscovered in the most sudden and surprising way. It is the story of hope and sorrow, of faith and gratitude. It is the story of patience and passion. It's the story of romance when least expected — when two pure hearts most needed to find joy.

Always in My Heart

Dedication

This book is dedicated to the memory of Jim Ragano and Ruth Gorius, beloved spouses of Margo and CJ. We talk about them frequently with thoughts of wonderful and enjoyable times spent over the years. Jim and Ruth loved us deeply, as we did them and they were dedicated to making us happy. We believe Ruth and Jim would be pleased with the happiness Margo and CJ have found with each other and will be sharing for the remainder of our lives.

Acknowledgements

Special thanks to Becky Karush of lifestorycompany.com, who painstakingly read more than three hundred letters we had exchanged and weaved them into the writing of this romance novel. Becky worked under a tight timeline to finish this project as it was meant to be a wedding gift to Margo. Becky is a freelance writer and specializes in personal stories.

Special thanks go to Doreen McAllister for managing this project in its entirety. Doreen worked closely with the writer over several months to coordinate the project, keeping it on schedule and managed a proofreading staff, all the while attending to her regular work and home responsibilities. We are indebted to Doreen for her attention to managing the details of this undertaking.

We also wish to acknowledge Sharron Francis for her role in reconnecting us. She knew us in high school and has stayed in touch with us throughout the years. Sharron more than anyone had a suspicion that the feelings we held for each other, although dormant, could be rekindled.

And finally we want to thank Georgette Feutren and Martha Gonzales, teaching companions of Margo. Martha was once her principal. These two people took the time to help with the final editing. We are extremely grateful for their interest and expertise.

I could not have compiled the letters and notes that formed the background for this book if it were not for Margo and her very close and dear friends. I have met many of them, and they all have played an enormous role in her life. They have been there when she needed them the most, and all of her close friends have contributed to her happiness.

CJ Gorius
June 1, 2013

Always in My Heart

Inspired by the love story of

CJ & Margo

They seemed to come suddenly upon happiness as if they had surprised a butterfly in the winter woods.

—Edith Wharton

Part One

Chapter 1

*C*onrad Holbrook leaned forward on the ski lift, pushing slightly against the metal bar that held him in place on the narrow plank. Below him, the snow-packed slope rose up faster and faster to meet his skis. He'd done this ten thousand times before, gliding in one smooth motion off the lift and onto the mountain, swooshing and carving the steep run until he was all speed and movement and joy.

This time, he felt a catch in his throat as he prepared to disembark. He wasn't scared, exactly — he knew too well how to manage himself on these New Hampshire slopes — but the sun, fierce and clear on a mid-November Saturday morning, glanced so sharply off the fresh powder that he couldn't tell for a second where the air stopped and the mountain began. Am I going to fall? He thought. Where am I going to land? Dear God, where am I going to land?

His mouth went dry and he squeezed his sparkling blue eyes shut. Tall and fit, looking nowhere near his 72 years, Conrad tensed all the muscles in his stomach and legs. Ben, his son, slid off the chair at the same time and met the mountain with confidence and grace. In his mind's eye, Conrad saw his daughters, Suzanne, owner of an internationally renowned thoroughbred stable, and Lynne, CEO of her own home and gardening supply business. His children were so brave and strong, his stalwart protectors since his wife, Laura, died six weeks ago after a long illness. They called him every day to check in, to make sure he was eating, to encourage him to get outside, to help him stay steady as possible after losing his companion of 49 years. Conrad saw Laura, then, as she'd been at the end, and as the young woman he married, and he felt blankness edged with terror band his chest.

Help, he thought. His Catholic faith had guided him through dark times before, and he prayed now that it would carry him across this unexpected, grief-filled gulf.

A few chairs back on the lift, a woman laughed suddenly, a peal as clear as a Christmas bell. Conrad smiled to hear it, his serious, handsome face brightening into a guileless boy's grin, and he found that he could breathe again, and that the cold air felt wonderful. He swung the metal bar away just before his skis hit the slope. He let the lift push him gently forward, and then he kicked once to catch up to his son.

The woman's laughter echoed in his ears. *Where have I heard a laugh like that before? He* thought. He replayed it, the loveliness of it, with sadness beneath that allowed for joy. As he maneuvered to the black diamond run, he stopped, face to the sun.

"Mariella," he said. His cheeks flushed red from wind. "That's how Mariella used to sound."

Conrad had received the first email from Mariella Cuore two weeks before Laura passed. He wasn't expecting to hear from her, then or ever. He'd barely thought about his high school sweetheart since he graduated 54 years ago from Clementskill North High School in Western Massachusetts.

It was the Internet, of all things, that bridged the long gap. During Laura's last months, Conrad kept family and friends apprised of her ups and downs on a social networking website for people coping with illness. Lucinda Barrett, a former Clementskill classmate, followed his daily posts. She and Conrad had reconnected two years earlier at the funeral of her brother Glenn, a close friend of Conrad's. She didn't expect Conrad to be at the service, but he made the nine-hour trek to pay his respects to his old friend.

Lucinda was a generous and savvy woman who cared for her large, complicated family, volunteered regularly at her beloved church, and even managed to run her own personal consulting business out of her home in upstate New York. She loved everyone she met, even those she didn't always like (her mechanic tried her patience sorely). She saw the good in people. In their sorrows and trials, she sensed their potential for happiness.

One day, she logged onto the website to see how Conrad was holding up. She knew him to be a serious, amiable, and steadfast man, and it broke her heart to see him and his family suffering. It was unpleasant, and sometimes impossible, to believe that their generation was now, officially, old; in the midst between sleeping and waking, high school memories felt close enough to touch. She felt that bright young girl in her blood still. She saw those teenage dreams glimmer in the eyes of her oldest friends.

A tough night, Conrad had written at 3 a.m. *Laura sleeps off and on, thirsty and sore, sometimes forgetting who she is or where we are. Your letters help us. I am grateful for your kind words and prayers. Especially those of you who have been through this. It helps us know that we aren't alone.*

Lucinda wrote a short, encouraging note, said a heartfelt prayer, and checked her email before tending to the day's many tasks. When she saw the name at the top of her inbox, she gasped, laughed, then tilted her head to the side, thinking. Mariella Cuore. A shiver zigged up the back of her neck — the time-tested sign that she was about to make something important happen — and she hit "Reply."

Darling Mariella,

Do you remember Conrad Holbrook? I'm sure you do. I remember how sweet the two of you were at his eighteenth birthday party, dancing to "All I Have to Do Is Dream."

He became a businessman and salesman, always great with numbers, you know. So handsome, and always good with people. Right now he's in the middle of caring for his wife who is gravely ill — too many of us know this suffering, so sad to say — and I think a note from you would be a welcome thing. Especially after losing Quincy three years ago and coming through that hard time. He might find some comfort and wisdom in what you have to say.

You were such good friends back in the day, even if he did break it off. Fifty-four years is definitely enough time for it all to be "water under the bridge"! ;-)

Lucinda sent her letter off.

It was very kind and thoughtful that first note from Mariella. Conrad remembered it as he carved wide arcs down the run, drawing his elbows tightly to his torso. He wasn't sleeping much those days, but even exhausted and mentally foggy he recognized the warmth and music of the girl he'd taken to Senior Prom so long ago.

Conrad...It has been such a very long time...I write this only to let you know that you and Laura and your family are in my prayers...Three years ago my husband, Quincy, was diagnosed with pancreatic cancer...such a shock...he passed away 8 months later. We thought we had so much more time together. It was not to be. Just a wee bit of advice...use this time to share, love, talk, remember...make the most of the days you now have...

Lucinda wrote and told me about Laura's situation. I am so sorry and saddened. Life is so very unpredictable. I continue to try to figure out God's plans...I am still working on that, but I have faith. Someday I will truly understand...

Do take care. Stay strong for yourself. She is a very lucky woman to have you by her side.

Warmly,

Mariella

In the shock of Laura's passing, Conrad didn't write back. He almost forgot about the letter entirely until his phone rang early Tuesday night last week. Conrad had sent a note to Lucinda earlier in the day asking if she had time to talk. She had been through this with the passing of her brother the year before and he hoped she might have some advice on how to cope.

"Hello old friend," a cheerful voice sang. "How are you holding up?'

Conrad smiled. He was sitting on the couch opposite the warm stove in his family room, watching the night fall over his snow covered lawn, the bare trees, the lead-blue sky. He was not an idle man; he had worked hard and well his whole life. But this minute, he was lonely, and he sat still.

"Lucinda," he said. "It's nice to hear from you."

They talked for an hour. Lucinda knew the toll and complicated blessings of caring for a very ill, beloved spouse. She had faith, though, in all things tending toward the good, and she encouraged Conrad to stay positive as he recovered and grieved.

As they were beginning to say their goodbyes, she cleared her throat and struck a casual tone. "So, did you ever hear from Mariella Cuore?" She knew he had; Mariella sent word of the email the day after she'd sent it. Lucinda wanted to know what Conrad thought about it.

"Oh, yes, I did," he said. The note popped into his mind in its entirety. "I was pleasantly surprised. You told me at Glenn's funeral you'd seen her, but besides that, I hadn't had more than a passing thought about her for 54 years. Suddenly I was reading her letter and it was like some conversation we'd started back then was still going on. Really, quite something."

This was perhaps the longest thought Conrad had uttered in several weeks. His own liveliness surprised him. He observed the surprise as if from a distance, wondering if it was okay to feel a sliver of sweetness so close to Laura's passing. To his greater surprise, he felt peaceful when he thought of his wife.

Lucinda tried to hide the smile in her voice. "Conrad, dear, that's no wonder. You two were very sweet together in high school. We all thought you'd come to some sort of agreement, but, well, we were stupid and young. We had no idea what was in store for us."

Conrad laughed sadly with her. "You told me that she'd lost her husband. She mentioned it, she said pancreatic cancer. It sounds like she's been through a lot."

"She has. Oh, she has walked down in the valley for some time now." Lucinda clucked her tongue in sympathy. "But she's very strong and wise. She has a lot to share." She held her breath, not wanting to push Conrad but willing him to say what she hoped to hear.

Conrad ran his hand over the nubbly arm of the sofa. He felt all the bumps and ridges, like a little earth beneath his palm. It was so nice to talk with Lucinda, a woman his age who understood the weight on his heart. Maybe Mariella could be a friend, too. "Do you think she would mind if I gave her a call?" he asked.

With a coolness belying her grin, Lucinda told Conrad that she thought Mariella wouldn't mind that at all.

He turned on his computer after he bid Lucinda a grateful good night. He found Mariella's note and settled his fingers on the keyboard to compose his reply.

The words came to him quickly. His own candor surprised him, the third surprise of what had looked to be a dreary night. It was easy to tell the truth to her.

I think I am in for a real change in my life that I had not prepared for, he wrote. I now can feel what you have gone through and are going through to try to recover from the loss of your spouse. Please believe me when I say that I am so sorry to hear about the loss of your husband and the burden you are left with to adapt to the sudden awareness that you are without your lifelong companion.

I had a long talk with Lucinda earlier. She is so positive and cheery I really appreciated her perspective on things. If it is OK with you, I would like to give you a call sometime to see how your life is going and how you are coping. Let me know. Regards, Conrad

On the mountain, Conrad slowed as the sprawling base lodge came into view at the bottom of the last, sweeping slope. He'd sent his email Tuesday night. Now it was Saturday, three and a half days later — an eternity in the digital age — and no word from Mariella.

Ben pulled up next to him. "You alright, Dad?"

Conrad put a half-smile on his face. "I've been training since August for ski season and my legs still feel like rubber bands."

Ben nodded. His father seemed a bit distracted. He and his sisters had kept a close watch on him since mom died, but Ben didn't want to press him too hard or invade his privacy as he grieved. Ben also knew that getting out on the mountain together was one of the best ways he could love and support his father. Skiing was a special and important time for both.

"I know. Twenty inches of new snow and a sunny morning....ideal skiing conditions, right Dad?" Ben knocked one of his ski poles against his father's ski and grinned. "Tell me again why you and Mom never settled in Colorado?"

Conrad gave a little nod. "Well, we were in the French Alps when you were born. That was skiing! And when we settled in New England to start the specialty flower business — remember how hot we had to keep the greenhouses for the Peruvian *Phragmipedium kovachii* orchid, the one your mother loved? — winter was still a nine-months-a-year thing. Remember when you were a kid? Even in the 1980s you could count on the snow."

"Shoveling out the driveway, I remember that," Ben said. "And the greenhouses. And the bulkhead. And the mailboxes. And the propane tanks. Tell me again why you and mom didn't have more boys?"

Conrad laughed out loud. "That's what I said to my father when I was a kid. But your sisters worked just as hard as you did, Ben, right? They used to complain that you never had to do the laundry."

Ben shook his head. "Oh, Mom made me wash my own clothes. After I left a Hershey's bar in my back pocket and it ended up with the good sheets, she wouldn't touch my laundry for a year."

They laughed, and then an awkward sadness fell between them. They shuffled a little on their skis, knocking off clumps of snow, fiddling with a boot buckle. A pack of snowboarders, arms dangling arrogantly at their sides, skidded past them.

"You go on down, Ben," Conrad said at last.

Ben looked at his father. "You coming? It's getting cold. The weather app said it's supposed to get really cold later on."

Conrad shook his head. "Just letting the legs rest. I'll be right after you."

Ben hesitated, nodded, and kicked off toward the lodge. Conrad watched him navigate around the snowboarders and a group of little kids learning how to snow plow, around a woman talking on a cell phone and around a man, clearly a novice, tottering and flailing on skis as wide as Nebraska.

Every day since Laura's death, Conrad felt like that brave, uncertain man. You lived a whole life of success, of money and travel, of meeting presidents and prime ministers, and still, one day you stumbled into a barren world where you couldn't catch your balance no matter how hard you tried.

But that guy was trying. It would be nice, though, to find sure footing. It would have been so nice if Mariella had written back. Oh well.

Chapter 2

P *lease, please let it be at least 7:30,* Mariella thought as she lay in bed, eyes still closed. One hand rested on her yellow lab, Franco. He had been named Franco after Franco Harris, running back for the Pittsburgh Steelers.

She stroked his belly, which rose and fell in even breaths. Her dear little Franco, who kept her company, made her laugh when he cocked his head to the side as if solving a math problem, chewed up tissues from every trash can (a crazy fetish!), and upended the bathroom trash any chance he got — he was a good friend to her in those lonely days.

The light against her eyelids grew stronger. *Yes,* she

thought. *Yes! It's seven-thirty for sure. I just slept four hours in a row.*

She cracked an eyelid open and bravely turned her face to the slate-gray digital clock, the one Quincy had chosen, with sleek blue numbers on the digital face and about 40 different alarm settings she'd never been able to figure out. As with almost everything electronic or digital in the house, remote controls to garage door openers, Quincy had been the one who knew which buttons to press, which menus to scroll, which options to choose. Double that for the cars, the boat, the bank accounts, the chopping of the winter firewood for the fireplace. He took care of it all.

3:53, the clock announced with cool, infuriating certainty. She turned away and groaned, wanting for a moment to cry until her tired bones melted into the bed. It was hard enough to wake up alone day after day. Did she have to wake up so darn early?

She blinked. She inhaled and exhaled. With a hand on her sleeping Franco, she began to pray. God had seen her through Quincy's sudden onset of cancer, his sudden death, and the wasteland of grief and confusion that followed. Her faith lived in her backbone; it breathed with her lungs and beat with her heart. She believed she could find her way to the heaven of her faith.

Franco sneezed suddenly and sat up with an indignant look on his pert face. Mariella laughed, and the sound broke the tension into giggles she couldn't stop, like tiny glittery fireworks bursting in her belly. "Oh, you precious thing," she said, sitting up and rubbing his ears. "God sure gave me a blessing with you."

She slid her feet into the soft lavender slippers Quincy bought for her on one of their many stays in Italy, and pulled a cozy fleece blanket around her shoulders. Winter had been late coming to her corner of North Carolina, but this pre-dawn chill surely heralded snow. With a big breath, she stood and reached her arms over her head, then placed her hands on her hips and leaned forward to stretch the spot in her back that always kinked in the night.

"Best get moving," she said. "It's my day to tutor the children at church. And we have to help them get ready for the Christmas pageant."

She stumbled on the edge of the blanket, breaking her fall against one of the posters of the master bed. Her shoulder twisted, and she let out a little cry. She stood still for a long minute to catch her breath, waiting to see if deeper pain followed. The image of Quincy dressed as Santa Claus the year after they married filled her mind. She saw the children at the naval base where he was stationed gather around him, some hopping with happiness, some anxious or shy. She heard him ask a little girl with a lopsided ponytail what she wanted for Christmas. Mariella had been pregnant with their first son then, and she'd leaned against a pole draped with real fir boughs to rest her swollen feet. Let Christmas always be this sweet, she'd prayed, happily confident it would.

In her bedroom so many years later, she pressed her shoulder, moved it in a slow circle, and made her way downstairs when she realized that nothing hurt. She touched her cheeks, wet with her tears. Some days, everything hurt. That was the blessed, bittersweet way of life.

Franco waited for her in the kitchen, wagging his tail with the bearing of a prince. She fed him, let him out to mark the frozen azaleas officiously, and rewarded him with a treat upon his triumphant return.

"Let's check the email, Franco dear. It's too early to start breakfast," she said.

In the leather and wood-accented study, Mariella regarded the computer with her usual mix of helplessness and irritation. It was a Quincy purchase, of course, and he'd used it to do everything, absolutely everything. She stuck to email.

She pressed the beast's "on" button, and then clicked on her email program. She still felt like a toddler trying to pick up a greasy marble when she used the mouse, but the pleasure of correspondence with her friends and family trumped her fear. Besides, she reminded herself every time she sat before the bluish screen; she'd been a teacher on naval bases and at international schools for 30 years. If she could handle classroom after classroom of children around the world, she could put up with this blankety-blank machine.

She smiled when she saw that Lucinda had written. Oh, Elliot and Judy, too! And her sons, Danny and Michael. She was always thrilled to hear from her children and her beloved grandchildren. A newsletter from her church. A service reminder from her mechanic — time for an oil change for the car, another task Quincy handled during their four-decade marriage. Mariella frowned, jotting down the reminder in the datebook she kept on the desk. As she wrote in her looped and buoyant handwriting, lively and warm as her nature, the computer pinged. Wonderful! A note from Ellen sent off just three minutes ago, another casualty in the battle against insomnia!

She wrote long letters to Ellen, Lucinda and Elliot and Judy. They had been such good friends to her, before and after Quincy's death; she considered them family. They helped her learn how to use an ATM and pump her own gas, for Pete's sake! To Ellen she wrote about the tail end of a dream she remembered from yesterday, in which she'd been dressing for her high school prom, fastening her lustrous black hair with a soft headband and smoothing a carmine-colored lipstick over her lips. She'd felt both childlike and sensuous in the dream, happy because she could see with her 70-year-old eyes how beautiful she looked, and sad because she knew the dance would end before she was ready to go.

The computer pinged again. Could Ellen be writing back already? Mariella clicked over to her inbox. 'Conrad Holbrook' flashed at the top of her screen.

Mariella gasped and clutched the mouse. Conrad's name disappeared, sucked with the sound of crumpling paper somewhere into the bowels of the insane computer.

"No, no, no!" Mariella banged the mouse and the keyboard at once. Franco barked at her feet.

"Right-o, Franco," she said, touching him quickly on the top of the head. "Best stay calm and find out where in the world I made this email disappear to. I can't believe this! He wrote back."

Ten minutes later, she wrestled the letter from whatever hell dimension it was trapped in and clicked it open. A new window blossomed on her screen with the first words from Conrad since she was seventeen.

As she read, her wide, dark blue eyes filled with tears that shone on her lovely high cheekbones. Her old friend, her first love, was suffering, and she did understand, more than he could possibly guess. She recognized the teenager in his sad, careful sentences, the thoughtful, confiding, smart young man who'd talked with her about God and math and Mrs. Eldridge's horrible English assignments.

Mariella read Conrad's letter three times, then sat in a reverie while Franco licked her ankles. The past swished around her like the gowns she used to wear to those high school dances. Conrad had written and shared his honest feelings with her. She had to respond immediately, but what could she say? It had been so many years, and email never captured the fullness of her emotions. How could it express the swirl of happiness and sadness she felt right now?

She leaned forward and began tapping the keyboard like a robin pecking the ground on the first day of spring

— a phrase here, a thought there. Then the words began to pour. She ignored the twinge in her back, ignored the "ding" of the coffeemaker in the kitchen, ignored her cell phone and the splatter of early winter rain against the study windows. Her long, elegant fingers typed and typed. It had been 54 years; her dear friend was hurting, and she had so very much to say.

Dear Conrad,

I kind of don't know where to start... Of course Lucinda called to let me know about Laura... I do know this is a very sad time for you and your family, but Laura being at peace... please let that bring you some solace, comfort. I know when Quincy passed away I was so relieved for him, for his long struggle to end. The void was, and still is at times, horrendous, but time does help...

Grief isn't the same for everyone. Follow your heart. Don't let others tell you, 'enough already.' Hold on to your years together... Those good memories can give you strength and courage to move on, one step, one day at a time.

Conrad, there were so many things I had to learn, right down to how to put a DVD in the player. But guess what, God gave me the strength, the courage, the encouragement to move on slowly...

God's love holds me together every day. You have always had a deep faith — let this guide you. Know in your heart all you did for Laura. Setting up the family photos around her when she was very ill was a beautiful idea. Lucinda told me about that. What a marvelous, thoughtful thing to do... Wowowow, as I like to say.

In answer to your question, if you ever do feel like talking, venting, or have questions — call anytime. I don't want to intrude or overstep my boundaries, and I probably won't have all the answers, but I am a good listener.

These next few days may turn into a blur...but pace yourself...laugh as much as you cry, share lots of memories...it is so good for the soul. Life is short and very, very precious. My goal is to try very hard to make the best of every day with which I am blessed.

Do take care. Be patient and kind to yourself. You are and always were a warm, caring, kind and gentle man.

Warmly,

Mariella

She scrolled up the page to reread her words. She hoped it was okay, not too personal or pretentious. Goodness, she didn't want to sound like a whiner or a know-it-all. She hoped Conrad would find the friend he seemed to be looking for.

"Oh Franco," she sighed to the loving content dog. "Who am I kidding? I hope I've found a friend, too."

She smiled at the thought, the same bewitching smile that always caught Conrad's eye in high school. Sometimes he would run his thumb over her cheeks, his touch light as a wisp of hair. It gave her shivers then — and now, remembering. She'd been to operas the world over, sailed past the glaciers of Alaska, but plain old high school trumped the greatest wonders for sheer perfect feelings.

Mariella shook her head. Yes, her memories were so sweet they stung, but she'd never give them up. She just had to get herself moving.

"Treadmill, Franco," she cried, standing up so suddenly she startled him from his impromptu nap. "And then we'll tackle that darn vacuuming before I head to church."

She jerked the mouse to the 'Shut Down' tab and gave the old computer a fond pat, or at least a slightly less annoyed tap, as it ceased its whir. With lightness in her step, one that caused her Lab to raise a curious eyebrow at the very heel sweeping by his nose, Mariella began another in the long set of days without Quincy, without a living breathing reminder of her whole rich and swirling life. This time, though, she noticed the jaunty brightness of the lamp lighting the study, how it made the browns and reds in the walls and furniture richer and deeper. She heard the rain patter on the windows like children running fast through a field. She smelled the cozy coffee aroma lolling from the kitchen, and she noticed how she felt hungry all of a sudden for orange juice and buttered toast.

There was only one thing Mariella Cuore didn't notice the very early morning she wrote back to Conrad Holbrook; she never hit 'send.'

Chapter 3

W ould you like to go to the church hayride with me?"

Mariella Cuore looked up from her locker. The third period bell was about to ring and the halls were crazy. She couldn't tell who had spoken until a tall, gentle-looking boy stepped closer to her.

"The church hayride," the boy said. "Would you like to go with me?"

Mariella stared at him. "Hi Conrad," she said calmly, she hoped. Her friend Kaye Holbrook's brother was a grade ahead of her, a business and math whiz. He was so tall. His crew cut was so nice. He wore a blue sweater with a white collared shirt underneath. He was swell.

Her heart jumped into her throat and down to her shoes. "You mean the one this Saturday?"

The boy nodded. She saw that his left hand gripped his intermediate algebra textbook so hard his knuckles were white.

She smiled her biggest smile, sending him all the friendliness and warmth she could muster. He blinked, and then smiled back as his hand relaxed around the textbook; his eyes locked on her.

"I'd love to," Mariella said, sending up a quick prayer that her parents would agree to let her go. She was 15, hardly a child, but rules were rules. Girls couldn't just say 'yes,' even if the boy asking was the sweetest, kindest, gentlest, most handsome boy in the entire school.

"Great," he said, his voice cracking slightly with relief. "It'll be a blast."

He reached out and touched the back of her hand, looking surprised at his own daring. Normally Mariella would have backed away if a boy touched her so intimately — he was gorgeous, but she hardly knew him — but instead she turned her hand over and wrapped her fingers around his.

Palm to palm, they stood, splitting the rush of students around them. Mariella's heart pounded in her ears and in her chests, but she felt calm, too. Her breath came light and free.

The bell rang, and the boy pulled away, breaking into a run to his class. Mariella closed her hand as if to keep the warmth of his skin with her. She couldn't move from the spot. She didn't want to. *Geography!* hissed the sensible part of her brain.She gasped and snatched up her books and notes, running before Mr. Cleveler marked her tardy.

At the other end of the hallway, Conrad looked back over his shoulder. He saw a flash of the the girl's thick, black hair as she turned a corner and caught a glimpse of one slim ankle and simple black shoe. He looked at his hand, the one that had held hers, and pressed it to his heart. He never did girly stuff like this, but he couldn't help it. He just felt glad.

"Mr. Holbrook." Conrad stopped running and groaned. Only one voice in the whole school could sound so sarcastic and terrifying at once. *Vice-Principal Holloman.* "Students are not allowed in the halls when class has started, correct? And you have been a student here for nearly three years, correct? Am I to assume that in that time you have neglected to learn the most basic rules of comportment and decorum?"

Conrad turned around to face the vice-principal, who was dressed, as always, in a mustard-yellow suit with a pea-green striped tie and brown loafers that bore mysterious white splotches.

"No, sir," he said. He was a good student, he never broke the rules, but Vice-Principal Holloman could not be counted on for rationality.

"Why, Mr. Holbrook, do you insist on placing your hand on your chest in that obsequious manner? Is there a flag I cannot see to which you must imminently pledge your allegiance? Am I to assume henceforth that you have powers of extrasensory flag perception, or that you are too intellectually ill-equipped to believe in the ability of the heart to beat without the pressure of your club-like hand?"

Conrad looked down at his hand, indeed still pressed to his chest. Before he could check himself, he smiled. He looked back at Vice-Principal Holloman and, entirely without his consent, the smile turned into an enormous grin. *Oh jeez*, he thought. *That's detention til spring.*

The man in the mustard-yellow suit regarded the grin. He did not speak or move. Conrad was sure he was counting up the proper, very high number of detentions he would administer.

"Right, then," the vice-principal said at last. He pulled a small pad of paper from his pants pocket, retrieved a pen from his breast pocket, and scratched out a short sentence. "Get yourself to class. Give your teacher this note. Do not let me catch you malingering in these hallways again unless you desire to prove yourself more imbecilic than I already suspect you to be."

"Yes, sir," Conrad said. Was Vice-Principal Holloman sick? Invaded by aliens? He took the note and bobbed his head in what he hoped was respectful gratitude. He turned to go.

"Mr. Holbrook." Conrad turned back, utterly confused. The vice-principal was grinning at him. Conrad felt dizzy with disbelief.

"She must be a very special girl."

The Church of Saint Anthony hosted a high school hayride every October. Six wagons made a lazy loop through the small, rural town, each wagon packed with couples and groups of friends slipping and fidgeting on the itchy straw. Father Gregory drove off first with his big black gelding, and there was Thor, who pulled the wagon at such a fast clip that surviving a Thor hayride was a Clementskill High rite of passage. The other drivers, mostly local farmers, kept to a slower pace that suited conversation, and, if the moon slipped behind a cloud, clandestine kissing.

Conrad had been on the hayride twice before — his tailbone remembered his freshman year ride with Father Gregory and Thor — but he'd never gone with a girl. Usually he and his best friend, Paul Stoddard, sat on the tailgate of one of the wagons, and they competed to see who could name the most constellations the fastest, a game they'd played since fifth grade. That year they each had received an amateur telescope for Christmas. On their previous hayrides they'd talk with their other friends about homework, or go over Math Club business, or sing along when Father Gregory boomed out a rousing hymn from the lead wagon.

This year, he had a date. This year, Paul had a date. Paul stopped at Conrad's house an hour before they were due to walk to their dates' houses. They'd tossed around a football, and rooted around in the refrigerator.

"Always empty, buddy, always empty! No wonder I'm so skinny," Paul said, as he did every time he was at Conrad's.

They spent three solemn minutes combing their crew cuts and splashing aftershave on their naturally smooth cheeks.

On the quiet street in front of Conrad's house, the two friends stood, watching Venus grow brighter as the sunlight leached from the sky.

"Hey," Paul said.

"Yeah?" Conrad was thinking of Mariella's hair. He was thinking about the next Math Club competition in nearby Pittsfield. He was thinking about how the collar of his pale blue shirt scratched his neck just below his ear. He was thinking about Mariella's small, warm hand.

"Take this." Paul held out red and tan foil packet with a blue diagonal line across the front.

Conrad paled at the sight of it. "Um. It's just a hayride, right? Is Anne, um, is she, I mean, all that hay, and Father Gregory's right there . " He blushed. His voice dropped to a whisper. "Is Anne loose?"

Paul looked confused and hurt, about to sock Conrad in the shoulder for insulting his date, the brown-haired yearbook staffer, Anne Kitts. Then he looked down at the packet and laughed.

"You dolt. It's Sen Sen, not whatever you were conjuring up in your dirty mind.." He socked Conrad on the shoulder anyway. "You don't want to kiss Mariella smelling like roast beef and root beer, do you?"

Conrad pocketed the candy breath mints, steadfastly staring at the ground. "Roast beef and root beer sounds pretty good to me."

"Don't I know it. You ate everything on that plate before I could get any." Paul laughed again and knocked Conrad more gently on the arm. "We better go get the girls."

"Yeah," Conrad said. They walked for a minute toward Elm Street, where they would part ways. "Paul?"

"Yeah."

"Are you going to kiss Anne?"

The boys were silent for another block.

"I want to," Paul said at last. "I think. It could be terrible. It could be like Godzilla kissing Kim Novak."

"You and Kim Novak." Conrad rolled his eyes. "Way out of your league."

"A skinny kid's gotta dream," said Paul. He was quiet again. "Are you going to kiss Mariella?"

Conrad didn't need to think about this question. "Yes," he said.

"Good," Paul said, breaking into a jog and turning backward so he faced Conrad as he ran away from him.

"'Cuz you'd be an idiot not to."

Conrad ran to catch up. At Elm Street they waved goodbye, their conversation tucked in their pockets with the packets of Sen Sen, a talisman of their friendship and a reminder to be brave, no matter what happened with these girls.

Mariella peered through the yellow living room curtains and saw Conrad walking up Willow Street. She curled her toes up in her penny loafers, clutched the hem of her gray cashmere sweater, closed her eyes, and wondered for one frantic moment if she should run out the back door. Linda, her younger sister, had teased her for wearing cashmere on a hayride, chiding that she'd come home looking like a scarecrow torn apart by crows.

"Leave her alone, Linda," their mother, Barbara, said, brushing Mariella's thick, shiny hair into a neat bob. "Remember when you went to the drive-in with David and you wore your shortest skirt?"

Linda pursed her lips and held a simple blue amethyst necklace to Mariella's neck. "This would look pretty on you, Mari. It brings out your eyes."

Mariella caught her mother's eye in the vanity mirror in her parents' bedroom, where each daughter primped before dates and big events. They smiled at each other, acknowledging Linda's swift change of subject, and Barbara reached out and patted Linda's shoulder gently. "You're right, love, that's just the color. Mari, you said Conrad's eyes are blue?"

Linda rolled her own eyes. "I believe she said they were 'the gentlest, kindest, sweetest, gorgeous-est ocean blue eyes God has ever in His most infinite wisdom created.'"

Mariella blushed. "Yes, Mom, I said blue."

Barbara gave her hair one last brush. "So you're presuming to know the wisdom of the Lord?" Mariella opened her mouth to apologize, then saw the corner of her mother's mouth twitch.

"You're teasing me too?" She put her cheeks to her face. "I must sound ridiculous."

Barbara laughed as Linda nodded. "You're just excited, sweetheart. I don't remember you getting this worked up when you went out with Wayne or Willie."

Mariella waved the names away, craning before the mirror to check the back of her skirt. "I was so much younger then. We were children playing at love. Conrad is a junior. And Kaye said he's very responsible around the house." She turned to face her mother as Linda rolled her eyes. "How do I look?" asked Mariella.

"Lovely, dear." Barbara's heart squeezed into her throat. Her eldest daughter was striking. She was exquisite.

She had no idea of her own beauty, or her innocence and natural reserve — some might say demureness.

She feared for her daughter, all her daughters, but especially her first, now fastening the amethyst around her neck. A young woman's reputation was so important; in her own youth she had seen girls ruined by their headlong rush into what they thought was love. She knew that her girls' faith was strong, and they drew strength from it and from the church and their prayers. They would likely tell her before trying anything rash, but still, the world was different from when she was a teenager. There were so many ugly temptations, from Hollywood stars wearing next to nothing on the 50-foot drive-in screen to that gang spitting and smoking outside the drugstore downtown. Young women had to choose carefully whom they dated and whom they loved, how much interest they expressed, how fully they responded to a boy's touch, how much danger they courted as they discovered their bodies and hearts. For a woman, Barbara knew, the man she married determined nearly everything about her life. She prayed that she had taught her daughters well.

"Remember, sweetheart," she said lightly. Teenagers, even the sweetest, could be tempestuous when parents meddled in their love lives. "You only deserve the best, a boy who will treat you with kindness and respect." Her words might as well have been cotton balls for all the giggling Mariella and Linda heard them as they danced about, preening in the mirror.

"Mariella, come show me how beautiful you look," bellowed her father, Charles, from the bottom of the stairs. Barbara smiled and began cleaning up the vanity as Mariella and Linda ran to him, pulling along their younger siblings, Rosie and George, in their wake. As long as Charles had anything to say about it, no boy would dare tread the front step if he treated Mariella like anything less than a queen.

It took Conrad most of the walk to the churchyard to recover his wits after meeting her mother and father and two sisters and brother. All of them eyed him with a powerful skepticism as he answered her father's questions about his schoolwork, family, church, extracurricular activities, career goals, and thoughts on Cuba, Gigi, and the death of Pope Pius XII. When they finally closed the front door behind them and began to walk, Mariella beamed at him.

"He really liked you," she said.

Conrad helped Mariella up the step-stool to the wagon, settling with her next to Paul and Anne and across from Daniel and Ellen, a cheerleader friend of Mariella's. Most of the kids were there as couples, Conrad noticed, which made him more comfortable, because he and Mariella wouldn't stand out. This also made him more nervous, because everyone was very, very quiet.

Paul caught Conrad's eye and grimaced. The young people sat like they were in Sunday Mass until the wagon hit a long patch of washboard ruts on an old dirt road. Up and down they bounced and jounced, on and on and on, fighting not to fall on top of each other.

Finally the driver, the dairy farmer Mr. Sloane, hollered back, "You kids alive back there?" They began to giggle, and then laugh even harder when they hit another set of ruts that jiggled their laughter like Jell-O. Paul looked at Conrad again and grinned.

"Oh my," wheezed Mariella. She held her stomach, trying to catch her breath, tears leaking from her eyes. "This is just so silly, isn't it? Oh wowowow, I don't know when I've laughed so hard."

Moonlight burst from behind a ragged cloud as she spoke. Conrad watched her bloom in the soft flash, the way her dark eyebrows arched beautifully, the way her hair kissed her temples. He saw how the corners of her lips dimpled gently beneath her high cheekbones. How smooth her skin was. How delicately she held her hands in her lap. Most of all, though, as Mariella lifted her face to the moon, he saw she was full of feeling, and was gorgeous.

"It's a nice night," he said. He didn't know what else to say.

"It is, isn't it?" Mariella said, brushing futilely at the hay that covered her gray sweater. "It makes me feel like I'm in a fairy tale. Like princes on white horses should be galloping by, or like magical birds are going to fly down and grant wishes and we'll all live happily ever after. But it's spooky, being out in the dark with the moon, like you just don't know what could happen around the next corner. It's kind of delicious." She ducked her head. "Oh, I'm talking too much. I don't mean to hog up all the time."

Conrad shook his head. "No, you're exactly right. That's how I feel too. Nights like this are like dreams. I've never known how to put that into words, but when it's really dark and the moon comes out, it's like you get to be a different person, almost, like all the secret parts of you that you didn't even know were there come out. It's like, you get to be who you are in Math Club and you get to be sort of, sort of..." he fumbled and trailed off, trying to figure out what he meant.

"Magical," said Mariella.

Conrad gaped at her. "Exactly. Yeah. You get to be magical, that's it exactly." He thought for a second. "I'm glad you said you would come out with me, Mariella."

She smiled at him. "I'm really glad too."

Conrad nodded. "Me too," he said. He curled his hand around the packet of Sen Sen.

Chapter 4

S urprise!

Mariella jumped up from behind the sofa in her living room. All the partygoers threw big handfuls of confetti in the air. Streamers, confetti, and glittery whirligigs showered down on Conrad, whose kind, intelligent face was agog with happy shock. Paul and Glenn Barrett, Lucinda's brother and a good friend who had starred in "Midsummer Night's Dream" alongside Conrad, popped up a moment after the rest of the guests and poured a bucket of kidney beans over his head while leading everyone in a round of "For He's a Jolly Good Fellow."

The crowd watched as Conrad walked straight to

Mariella. Confetti stuck to his crew cut like oversized snowflakes.

"You did this?" His grin was so goofy, and his eyes so bright she could have cried.

"Yes," she said. "Are you happy?" She knew he was, but she wanted to hear it out loud. She hoped she wasn't being too pushy. She'd been planning this 18th birthday celebration for weeks, secretly sending out invitations, collaborating with Paul and Anne on decorations and food, asking Conrad's mother to help keep him busy during the morning of the party so she and all his friends could gather without Conrad suspecting anything. She loved creating a wonderful event for her boyfriend. She would fly to the moon and bring back cheese for the guy who'd given her his class ring.

In answer, Conrad pulled a foil packet from his pocket and snapped a small candy into his mouth. Mariella blushed from her hairline to her knees. They'd been together almost a year now. She knew what came next.

Conrad placed one hand at her waist and the other on her shoulder blade. He leaned in. "I am happy," he whispered, and he kissed her. The whole room erupted in cheers, whistles, and more than a few half-thrilled, half-jealous tears.

The rest of the party passed in a happy blur, like every day Conrad and Mariella had spent together since that church hayride. Conrad read all his cards, opened presents, played a round of table hockey with his best friends. He ate three bowls of Mariella's special Italian wedding soup. Later, Anne Kitts put on an Everly Brothers record, and all the couples danced in slow circles in the middle of the living room, the couches and chairs pushed to the walls.

Mariella squeezed Conrad's hand when "All I Have to Do Is Dream" ended, and she walked to the couch where Lucinda and MaryJo Devons were gesturing for her. They each moved over to make room for Mariella in the middle, crossing their legs and leaning toward her.

"It's a great party, Mar," said Lucinda. "just wait till he sees the present you got him."

MaryJo shook her head. "I don't know which he'll like better, the framed picture of the two of you from the Prom last year, or the desk set. All leather, the fountain pen, the date books and assignment books and that little book of prayers with the color of the cover matching the leather — it'll be perfect for his first semester at Wheaton."

Mariella beamed at them, happier than they guessed as she thought of the loving and encouraging notes she'd tucked into the date books and assignment books, and the handwritten psalms she'd folded into the little book of prayers.

"Are you worried about next year?" Lucinda knew her tender-hearted friend cared deeply for Conrad and would miss their walks to schools, their lunches and locker conversations, terribly. She'd known Mariella for a long time and worried for her happiness, even though they were the same age.

Mariella wove her fingers through her generous, loving friend's fingers. Lucinda always looked out for her, ever since they met in homeroom their first day of high school. The moment she stepped into the classroom, Mariella had dropped the entire contents of her knapsack on the floor. Eddie Maynard stood on his desk and started clapping until Mrs. Dartmoor gave him a detention, and Mariella could hardly gather the pencils and notebooks from her trembling hands.

Lucinda watched from a desk three rows away. Suddenly she stood up, grabbed her own knapsack. As she moved to help Mariella retrieve her things, she accidentally-on-purpose dropped her books and papers on the floor, too. The sudden, doubled mess surprised Mariella out of her embarrassment. She sat back on her heels, pressed her hands to her cheeks, and smothered a wild giggle. "We're all in this together," whispered Lucinda with a wink, and she kneeled next to Mariella and scooped up her books.

In the living room the day of Conrad's surprise birthday party, Mariella smiled at Lucinda. "Of course college will be a change for us," she said. "But we get along so well. We talk about everything and it's so easy and fun." She disengaged her hand from Lucinda's and looked at the class ring Conrad had given her. It looked solid and important, like she was a queen and the ring was her official seal.

MaryJo picked up Mariella's hand and brought the ring closer to her face. "It looks good on you. When Stu gave me his ring last year, I felt beautiful! MaryJo dropped Mariella's hand. She wasn't vain. Editor of the school literary magazine and a top student, she had big ambitions for herself. She was pretty and petite. She knew, too, with a precocious intelligence that had annoyed and impressed more than one teacher, that being pretty and petite could be a good thing. People admired her for her mind; she won them over with her wit and good humor. So far, the combination had allowed her to become the school literary editor, work six hours a week at the Clementskill *Daily Telegraph* as an assistant copy editor, not just a coffee girl, and win a scholarship for a summer term for high school juniors at Radcliffe College. It was true she was lonely sometimes, especially after Stu left for Rutgers. He had big dreams, too, and they'd spent whole afternoons spinning out tales of their grown-up lives in New York and Boston and London and, one daring day, Paris and Senegal. They'd made each other laugh so hard, trying to imagine themselves in impossibly far away Africa, that Stu had literally popped a button on his plaid button down shirt. Talking, laughing, kissing — time with Stu had been like a poem. The day he left, they didn't talk so much. No matter how hard they had looked around them, they never saw a marriage where the husband and wife both strove to make a name for themselves in the world. For their worldly conversation, and all MaryJo's sophisticated reading, they didn't even bother to imagine a real future together. That night was the one time MaryJo allowed herself to cry.

"Oh MaryJo," said Mariella, "I'm pretty sure school literary editors can wear rings."

Mariella looked at her. "MaryJo! do you hear from him ever?"

"I saw his mother after Mass last week," said Lucinda, casting a quick glance at MaryJo. Some topics were best left to rest. "But Mariella, have you and Conrad talked at all about next year?"

"He showed me the course catalog, and we read over the classes he wants to take," Mariella said. "Advanced trigonometry for one. I said he ought to join the acting club there. He was so good in 'Midsummer Night's

Dream.' I don't think I've ever seen a more perfect Lysander."

"Okay, Hermia." MaryJo rolled her eyes. "Your two characters just happened to end up married at the end of Act V, n'est ce pas?"

Mariella blushed but held up her chin proudly. "No, I thought he was a good Lysander because he was an excellent actor."

"And so he was," Lucinda agreed, re-knotting the crimson silk kerchief she wore around her neck. "He really took to the stage like a natural. Not so much when we went 'camping,' right?"

Mariella burst out laughing. "Oh, wowowow, that was a funny night."

MaryJo held her head in her hands. "What about square dancing? It took us all so long to get that one dance. I thought the caller was going to fall off the stage."

The girls began talking all at once, remembering double dates, school talent shows and hockey games, ice skating, drive-in movies, Friday night dances, the Prom club meetings and church suppers.

"You and Conrad really do a lot of things together, don't you," Lucinda said when they quieted. "Like you said."

Mariella nodded. They'd done everything you could in Clementskill, but she liked the simple times the best. On Sundays, Conrad would drive them up into the hills, down the back roads and through neighboring towns. They talked on and on, words and ideas and feelings coming in such an easy rush that sometimes they forgot the time. Conrad had to break the speed limit to get back home before supper. The conversations made her feel like God had created each with the other in mind. Sometimes they stopped on the back road, and Conrad would unwrap a packet of the Sen Sen. Mariella could hardly breathe; her whole body tingling, knowing he was about to kiss her.

"I hope you and Conrad come to an arrangement," Lucinda whispered as the three finally left their cozy sofa nest to rejoin the party. "I hope it all works out in the end."

As much as Mariella loved her friend, she listened with only half an ear, thinking of the birthday present and of the three-layer chocolate cake she would soon serve .She also wanted to dance with Conrad again, so she figured she ought to go stand next to him so he would ask her.

"It always works out in the end, Lucy," she sang as she skipped away. "Always in the end."

Paul Stoddard was going to California Institute of Technology next year. The acceptance letter had come on Monday, six days ago.

"CalTech's in Pasadena," he was saying to the boys clustered around him. "Ten miles from Los Angeles."

"So basically you'll be living in Hollywood," said an awed Danny Flanders. "Are you going to meet Kim Novak?"

Paul appeared to consider the questions seriously, shooting a barely perceptible wink to Conrad before replying with his dryest deadpan. "Probably. CalTech does sponsor regular lunches with her. But between all my lunches with Nobel laureates and all my dinners with the nuclear scientists from Los Alamos, Kim and I won't have much quality time."

Danny looked impressed until the other boys nudged him, grinning, and he rolled his eyes at Paul.

"Yeah, I'm kidding, Dan-o. But it's true, I think it's true, I think," Paul fumbled his words, a rare slip for him, betraying his own awe at what fate had chosen for him. "It's true that CalTech will keep me pretty busy."

As the other boys drifted away, Conrad turned to Paul. "Why didn't you tell me you got in?" He spoke quietly.

Paul looked abashed, another unusual event. Paul was confident and quick, the emcee for the senior talent show and the school math genius (he and Conrad competed for that regard). He never let his feelings overwhelm him. "Sorry. It's no big deal, I just — "

"It is a big deal," Conrad said, impatience creeping into his normally collected voice. "Your dad must be really happy. Your mom must be pretty much turning cartwheels. You've worked really hard for this. It's a big deal." He caught his breath. "Good for you. I mean it."

Paul gave him a grateful glance. "I couldn't believe it at first. I know I talk a good game, but I didn't think they'd accept me. Then we were working on the party, and I didn't want to break the mood. Mariella's been over the moon getting this shindig together. I would have waited till tomorrow, but my mom told Danny's mom, and that was that."

Conrad nodded. He looked away from Paul. "Mariella did a pretty good job. I had no idea."

Paul regarded him; his amused detachment returned to him. "You moron," he said. "She loves you."

He pushed off the chairback he'd been leaning on and made his way across the room, where a now blindfolded Danny was swinging haphazardly with a foam bat at a green and yellow pinata hanging from the ceiling. Conrad took a sip of punch.

"Hey there." He heard Mariella's soft voice behind him, and he relaxed, a smile loosening the clench across his forehead. He turned and folded her into a hug, sinking into a chair and pulling her onto his lap.

"Paul's going to CalTech," he said.

Mariella leaned against his chest and clasped her hands together on her lap. "Jeez. That's really far away. Did you just find out?"

Conrad nodded. "He's wanted to go to a school like this since he was in second grade. His dad went to MIT, so, yeah."

Mariella waited for a moment before speaking. "If it were me I'd be a little sad, too. If my best friend were going across the country. After all the good times we've had in high school." She put her forehead against his temple. "We're growing up and becoming adults, but we don't want anything to change either. I'd be a lot sad."

"That's it exactly," he whispered. "Everything's changing. They sat in gentle silence as the party swirled around them. "But God will take care of us." He blinked. "Right?"

Mariella nodded. Tears swelled to her eyes. He sounded like a little kid, and she loved him so much for trusting her with his scared self. "Definitely. And I'll always be here for you, too. Always."

She sat up, shook the sadness away, and pointed across the room. Lucinda and Anne were carrying in the chocolate cake lit with eighteen cheerfully sputtering candles. "And now we have to get you some cake," she said. "I know you've got English homework and your mother wanted you home by 7:30. She told me," Come on!"

She jumped up and joined the crowd as they began to sing 'Happy Birthday.' Paul was right. She loved him. So why, just then, did it cross her mind that God's plan for them might be stranger and more complicated than they thought?

In the meantime Conrad felt like he was looking down at the party from the top of the moon, seeing his girlfriend and his best friends. Mariella waved at him to come blow out the candles, and for the first time, he didn't beam back at her smile. He wouldn't leave for college for months, but part of him was already gone.

Chapter 5

*M*ariella pushed herself as close to the passenger side door as she could, as far away from Conrad sitting in the driver's side. His hands gripped the steering wheel. Inside the car was silence. Outside, the last of the spring peepers hollered the final booming chords of their rambunctious love song.

She removed his class ring from her necklace. She held it with her thumbs and forefingers, twisting it so that the streetlight glinted off it. The metal was cold. It couldn't even hold the warmth of her skin, and she'd been wearing it night and day all through the winter and spring. It was just metal, and it didn't belong to her anymore.

She placed the ring on the dashboard. Conrad looked at it and sighed.

"You're being really dramatic, Mariella." He leaned back in his seat and moved his hands to the bottom of the steering wheel. "It's simple. Like my mom said, I'm going to college in a few months. It's better for both of us to end this now. We have no idea what the next four years will bring. My mom said it's better to break it off now before it gets complicated. You'll see next year when you go to college. I wish you wouldn't be so upset."

Mariella couldn't find a word to say. Her whole body hurt. She forced herself to speak. "It's okay. Your mother is right. It's not like we were ever going to get married. You shouldn't be tied down. What a silly idea. Ha!"

"Exactly," Conrad said. He knew he was doing the right thing breaking up with Mariella, but it was going so badly, the words slipping out of his control. Obviously, he couldn't ask Mariella to help him figure out what he felt, and Paul, who would see the problem and its answer at once, was across the country visiting CalTech. He meant for this to be straightforward. His mother had made it seem so clear.

Corinne Holbrook had asked her only son to sit with her in the dining room after Mass last Sunday. With the bold spring sun making sharp shadows across the heavy oak table, she crossed her legs and laced her fingers together in her lap. Conrad wondered if she'd found the cigarettes at the bottom of his t-shirt drawer. Or maybe his sisters had finally tattled about his taking the car in the night with Paul to catch a midnight showing of 'Vertigo.'

"How is Mariella?"

The question threw him. "Mariella? She's great. She loves cheerleading, she's a top sales person for the magazine drive at school, so that's good. She's great," he said again. His mother always treated Mariella well, chatting in the kitchen or asking for her help in the flowerbed or with the little kids during Sunday school. "I mean, she talks a lot about next year. How we'll visit each other. A lot, but she's great."

Corinne regarded him, and then looked down at her hands. She had prayed through much of the service for the wisdom and skill to say to her son what she needed to say. He was a gentle boy, talented and sheltered in the safety of his home and school and this small town. Mariella was a wonderful, lovely and loving girl; even her daughters approved of her heartily. Kaye, especially, sang Mariella's praises as a kind, loyal friend. Corinne knew the Cuore family was both devout and devoted to the community. But the children were just that: children, all so young, so untested and young.

"The two of you have had a sweet time together," Corinne said. "As your mother, it's been a pleasure to see you have such a good friend."

"Thank you?" Conrad couldn't keep the question out of his voice, even though it made him sound rude. "I mean, thank you."

"But you are leaving for Wheaton very soon. You are bright, Conrad, and you have a great deal of potential to discover. I know Mariella's friendship has meant much to you, but this isn't the time to have an entanglement that might hinder you as you begin your college studies. She'll be here, in high school, while you are meeting new friends and learning from new teachers. It would be unkind to lead Mariella on, thinking that you are committed to her alone when you are in fact involved in the world of college and all it has to offer."

She took a breath and looked straight at her son. His face was slack, his eyes locked on her with the trust and openness of the little boy he once was. This is the right thing to do, Corinne thought. Look at my boy, about to go out into this messy world. He doesn't need the responsibility of another person's heart yet. He'll find that in time. When it is time, he'll find love.

Around the corner, Kaye and her sisters, Margaret and Pam, crouched, listening hard. Kaye looked shocked and heartbroken, but Margaret and Pam weren't surprised at their mother's words. Disappointed? Yes, as Mariella was a swell girl, head over heels in love with Conrad and funny and spirited in her own right. But they knew their mother and how protective she was of her son, how much she and their father believed in their children's potential to succeed as adults.

Margaret wiped away two tears. Mariella and Conrad were perfect together. Besides, Mariella was her friend, too, and she doubted Mariella would want to spend time with her and coach her in cheerleading if Conrad broke things off. She wanted to run into the dining room and holler at her mother to let things be, to let Conrad and Mariella get married tomorrow and then everybody could live together in the house and nothing would ever have to change. But for all that Margaret adored Mariella and loved the picture of Conrad and Mariella in love; she was a practical girl, too. Her mother wouldn't let her out of the house for ten years if she butted in. It was so unfair; all Margaret could do was cry.

"You need to end your friendship with Mariella," Corinne said. "Your father and I realize that this might be painful for you, but it is the best course. It is best for you and for Mariella, too. You are going out tonight, correct?"

Conrad nodded.

"Tonight, then, should be your last date. A clean, swift break is the best for everyone. Do you understand?"

Conrad nodded. Graduation was soon. He would work as Mr. Glenderman's sales and marketing assistant at the Ford dealership this summer. His family would stay at the lake house in the Adirondacks for two weeks in July. There would be Lucinda's Fourth of July barbeque and the church square dance in August. Then he would leave Clementskill for college, forever. His mother was right. He needed to make a clean break so that when he left, he left high school behind. In a quiet part of his mind he barely knew was there, he was relieved that he didn't have to make the horrible decision to break Mariella's heart on his own. His mother was right.

"Okay," he said. "Yeah, that makes a lot of sense."

"Good," said Corinne. She longed to hold him as she'd held the baby, the five-year-old and the ten-year-old mourning the death of his pet turtle. She prayed he'd always have friends as good as Mariella had been, to carry him through the sorrows that would cut deeper than the loss of turtles and high school sweethearts. "Now go change your clothes." She stood up and rubbed his head. "The lawn isn't going to mow itself."

"It's simple," Conrad repeated in the car. Mariella hadn't anything on the long drive back to her house. Why did he drive all the way to Pittsfield to break up with her? This was awful. "It's simple, I keep telling you; it's simple."

"But don't you love me?" Mariella covered her mouth with her hand. She hadn't meant to let her true thoughts burst from her, but this was Conrad. She had no practice in keeping secrets from him.

"That really isn't the point," he said, which struck him as maybe not the nicest thing to say, but he had to be clear. Clean and swift, he thought. A clean swift break.

"What is the point?" Mariella couldn't help it; she was angry. It felt terrible. "Do you hate me?"

He didn't know how to answer. What was the clean and swift answer to a question like that?

Mariella paled. "You hate me." She began to cry.

"Now stop it, Mariella. Stop it. Just stop crying." He pressed on the accelerator as the road opened onto a straightaway. "Don't be pessimistic, alright? I don't hate you. You believe me, right? I don't hate you."

She choked back a sob and wiped her nose with the collar of her sweater as discreetly as she could. "I don't understand," she whispered.

Conrad felt his neck and cheeks grow hot. He so rarely got angry; he didn't recognize the emotion. He wondered if the air conditioning system of his father's car was on the blink, filling up the interior with hot air instead of cold. He didn't notice that his voice grew louder or that his foot began to press harder on the gas pedal.

"I've already explained it five times," he said. "Like my mom said, I'm going to college. Next year you're going to college. We don't want to tie each other down."

"You mean your mother doesn't want you to be stuck with me while you're off at school, and you're too nice to break up with me on your own," She was really angry now, and it almost felt good, at least better than being dumped by the best boy she'd ever known.

"My mother is right about a lot of things," Conrad said. The speedometer gauge crept higher, past 55, past 60. "But this isn't about her. A man can't let life just happen to him, don't you get it? A man has to choose his way. He has to take a stand and decide who he's going to be and what he's going to do and who's going to stand by him. He can't just let things happen to him. A man can't just let life happen to him."

Mariella turned to spit back the first venomous retort of her life — "You're no man," she meant to sneer — when through her furious tears she saw Conrad's jaw shaking from his effort not to cry. She understood then. All the fight went out of her.

"You're angry at Paul," she said. "Your best friend is leaving you behind."

Conrad took his eyes off the road looked at her with a sad, sweet tumble of loneliness and joy. She had revealed the truth of his mind to him again. I love you, he thought. Then he heard the car engine whine, and he realized he had pressed the gas pedal all the way to the floor.

Mariella clutched his arm. "Conrad, we're going too fast. Please, slow it down, slow it down. Please, stop the car, please."

The speedometer hit 85 miles an hour as the bad curve leading into Clementskill loomed a half-mile ahead. Conrad didn't think. He took his foot off the gas pedal and slammed both feet on the brake.

Even with their eyes closed, they both felt the car spin in a fast full circle, and then another, the tires shrieking and popping and cursing against the blacktop. They slid from the wide paved road into the soft embankment, the right side of the car sinking and slowing with the friction and the left side rising up like an indifferent wave. Mariella screamed.

And with that, the car was still. Upright, pointed toward home, barely off the road, and not moving at all. By God's or the highway department's grace, the width of the road had allowed them to spin mostly on the pavement, losing enough speed to keep the car from toppling when it finally hit the shoulder. The engine was even running smoothly, not even an idle hiccup.

Conrad and Mariella grabbed each other's hands. Mariella whispered a prayer of gratitude, Conrad another. A car drove past, the first since Conrad lost control, and he prayed again his gratitude that the road had stayed empty so long. When both were silent, Mariella pulled away. She felt a bruise rising on her elbow where it must have struck the door, but she didn't rub it or check for a scratch or scrape. She sat as straight as her shaking body would allow and folded her hands in her lap.

"I'd like to go home now," she said.

Conrad tried to even his breath. "I'm sorry."

She turned to look at him; her eyes filled with love and hurt. "I know," she said. "Conrad, please just take me home."

Chapter 6

June 1959

Dearest Conrad,

High school is coming to a close for you, but haven't you spent four wonderful years? You've participated in numerous activities and have made some wonderful friends.

College is just around the corner. You'll soon have to choose your vocation and settle down. I certainly wish you all the happiness any one person could wish to another.

I don't know where to begin to thank you for all the marvelous times I've spent with you. They have been wonderful experiences for me and I know I couldn't possibly forget them. We have had our quarrels, but you're still a very understanding person. We have done so many things and gone so many places together. I hate to see everything come to an end, but you must go your way and I must go mine.

Conrad, I sincerely mean it with all my heart when I say you are the most wonderful person I have ever met. I don't know quite what to say about our breaking up. In a way I think I've learned a lesson but I wish it hadn't been with you.

You don't have to worry about leading me on or will I stop talking about you, etc. My feelings inside can't change but my outward ways will and have.

I'll always think of you as a wonderful person who I talked with and one whom I had complete confidence and faith in. I was always able to talk with you and I *have hopes that sometime we'll understand each other and how much we meant to each other.*

Don't let this letter bother you, Conrad.

You're just a tremendous guy and I want you to know it. By the way, I still say that prayer I once gave you — silly, aren't I? (Only kidding about being silly.)

Conrad, as long as you keep your wonderful belief in God you'll easily become the successful person you wish to be and remain the wonderful person you are now. Don't ever forget this, Conrad, even if you forget everything else. I hope you always remain the same, sweet, gentle and religious person you are now. May God always be with you to lighten your path.

Very fondly with love,

Mariella

P.S. I sincerely hope that we will always remain the very best of friends.

P.P.S. I'm not being pessimistic about anything I said to you, Conrad. I'm sure you don't hate me!

Mariella set down her pen. That was everything she wanted to say. Since the night the car went off the road, she and Conrad had said 'hi' in the hallways. Their group of friends spent all their time together at and after school, so she'd been around him plenty. She just needed to share her heart with him once more, even if he never read the letter or lost it as soon as he read it. Then she could believe her mother when Barbara held Mariella and said the right man would find her in God's own time. Her mother promised she would have a wonderful life.

In the meantime, Mariella had senior year and college to look forward to, and whether she wanted to become a teacher or a maybe a nurse before she got married. She tucked the letter into a notebook and gathered up her school things. Yearbooks came out today. She'd do her darnedest to be the last one to sign his, and when she did, she'd paperclip her letter to the last page, the blank one after the 'Patrons' listings that no one ever paid attention to. He'd find it tonight or tomorrow or someday, long after he'd forgotten how he fell in love with her underneath the autumn moon.

Part Two

Chapter 7

C onrad didn't forget the letter right away. It took a couple of years before the yearbook drifted to the bottom of the bookshelves in his college dorm room and another couple before he packed it in a cardboard box labeled "High School." He shoved the box into a corner of his parents' basement during spring break.

He and Mariella even went on a few dates the summer between his freshman and sophomore years, just before she headed off to Berkshire State Teacher's College, but nothing came of it. Their conversations were pleasant, light-hearted, and enjoyable.

Mariella finally told him she thought it would be best if they kept things uncomplicated and stopped seeing each other. The last time he saw her was on her front porch. She said good luck, and he walked away.

By the time Conrad graduated from Wheaton, Mariella had faded into the general fond memory of high school and home and simple good times. He kept in touch with Paul, each of them writing a letter a month. One summer they took a fly-fishing trip with their fathers, memorable in that none among the four knew how to fly fish.

The world moved fast in the early 1960s. People were buying cars, watching color television, shooting spacecraft to the moon, inventing artificial turf and communications satellites and buffalo wings. Everything was possible for a young man with smarts who could work hard. After graduation, Conrad parlayed his experience at the Clementskill Ford dealership into positions of greater leadership at dealerships near Wheaton, and then Ithaca, where he attended S.C. Johnson Graduate School of Management at Cornell University part-time.

In 1962, he met Laura at a graduate student mixer. She was studying hospital administration at Cornell and living with her parents in nearby Corinth, where she'd grown up. From that moment on, he knew he was a grown-up, ready to commit himself fully to this beautiful woman, before his family, his community, and God. They married not long after they met, and Paul flew east from L.A. to be his best man.

The years rolled into each other, happy and busy, so packed with responsibility and discovery once the children came that Conrad never had the desire, let alone the chance, to look back. In 1969 he secured a job with Ford's international sales and marketing division, and for nearly 15 years he and Laura and the kids lived all over the world, Gstaad to Patagonia, meeting business leaders, politicians, artists and actors, as the American motor vehicle became a status symbol of power and taste. Conrad and Laura, both from small towns with tight-knit communities of good, solid people, made a strenuous effort to show their children the ordinary lives being lived outside the opera houses and hotel suites Conrad's work included. The family camped on a tiny beach in Costa Rica, making friends with the fishermen who trawled for sailfish and marlin every day. They walked quiet streets in Venice, the only sound the slap of water against the stained stone canals, and bought espressos from solemn-faced signoras in dark cafes (the kids spit theirs out and begged for gelato). They got out of their car and tried to help a shepherd in Bavaria herd his sheep away from the road and back into their field, but he ended up sending several foul-sounding curses their way when their efforts stranded three confused ewes on the far side of a neighboring and surprisingly deep brook. They didn't discuss religion often, but Conrad made sure they attended Catholic Mass in churches in Poland, France, Auckland and Rio. Conrad and Laura did their best to teach their children that hard work, family, and faith would see them through life better than riches alone.

The children were teenagers when the family settled in New England to start the specialty flower nursery. Conrad had earned his M.B.A. at the London School of Business during a three-year assignment in Britain, and though his colleagues thought his move from international sales to CEO of a New Hampshire nursery was anticlimactic, he knew it was the right decision. His children needed to put down roots. They needed to get their hands dirty in land they could love over time. They needed to learn the value of work and money and sweat. They needed not to be jet set travelers but ordinary children, before they took on the world themselves.

Conrad and Laura needed to slow down, too. For a long time they thought Laura's exhaustion was just jet lag, but in the last few years she got tired and stayed tired, no matter how many naps or baths they worked into the day. Starting a physical business like a nursery wasn't exactly a vacation they admitted one night, but it was a dream come true for her, and it didn't involve so many airplanes.

They kept the nursery running successfully until their children were through college. In the empty nest years, as the children married and settled into careers of their own, Conrad and Laura decided they'd had enough and sold the business to their favorite rare flower colleague. Suddenly at loose ends, they traveled here and there. They visited Paul on the West Coast, Laura's friends in Florida, work friends in Europe and South America. Conrad became involved in the emerging field of Internet security technologies, and he volunteered with an organization that helped would-be small business owners learn sales and marketing skills. Laura tended to her greenhouse and taught local school children about botany and ecology through the weird magic of orchids. Together Conrad and Laura visited their grandchildren as often as they could. Far too quickly, they agreed, they became young seniors, then turned into no-kidding seniors, and held hands as they approached the edge of no-going-back seniorhood.

Laura's perpetual tiredness was too severe to ignore now, try as she might. Conrad felt an ache in his own bones, but he knew it wasn't illness. It was dread.

About a year before she passed away, when they'd both become inured to morning med routines and emergency oxygen tanks, Conrad received word from his sister Margaret that Glenn Barrett, his high school friend and drama comrade, had died.

He arranged for trusted friends and neighbors to take care of Laura for three days. It was a nine-hour drive to Clementskill, where Lucinda Barrett was organizing the wake and funeral for her brother; Conrad felt compelled by something larger than nostalgia to make the trip. He hadn't thought much about high school in decades, but now he needed to pay his respects, both to Glenn and that old cache of memories.

Lucinda was shocked and touched to see him. Her face drawn, sorrow pulling down the corners of her eyes and slumping her shoulders, she still managed a genuinely enormous smile and hearty hug when he came up to her.

"Conrad Holbrook." She put her hands on his shoulders. "I haven't seen you in what, 40 years? The last time was when you came for your daughter's baptism, and Glenn was her godfather? You look not a day over 55." In truth he looked as worn out as she felt. "How are you? How are your kids? How's your wife — Laura, right?"

She inhaled sharply when she saw the look in his eye. "Got it. No need to explain, but if you want to talk about it, I'm here. We're all facing the same things now. We're all in this together, right?"

Conrad patted her shoulder. "Lucinda, you're quite something. We're at Glenn's funeral that you organized, and you're comforting me." He smiled weakly. "I'm okay. Laura's doing the best she can. How are you?"

Lucinda shrugged. "I think I'm getting kind of old. I look in the mirror, and I'm surprised when 25-year-old me isn't looking back. Glenn had a hard time at the end. My husband, well, he has good days and bad days. But the children are good. Business is good. Honestly, I don't have much time to look in the mirror, so that's probably a blessing."

Conrad nodded. He felt the same way when he had a moment to consider his life from a distance.

"But you know who I did see this year?" Her face brightened and her shoulders straightened. "Mariella Cuore! She's Sellesbury now, has been for forty-something years, but she's still Mariella, sweet as pie and tough as nails."

"Wow," Conrad said. He broke into a grin.

Lucinda laughed. "Four of us girls from high school had a mini reunion down at Mariella's house in North Carolina. She and her husband Quincy moved there from California after they retired, oh, ten or so years ago. We had a blast."

"They lived in California?"

"Well, it was either there or Italy or Uzbekistan. They did a lot of traveling up until the end."

Conrad's stomach sank. "So, her husband, her... Quincy?"

Lucinda looked wan again. "Yep. Two years ago. It hasn't been easy for her. She's doing better now."

A young woman walked up to Lucinda and hovered at her elbow, not wanting to interrupt their conversation.

"It's alright, Nell," Lucinda said. "I'm here. How can I help you, sweetheart?" She laid a hand on Conrad's arm and promised to find him before he left, then wrapped an arm around her niece's shoulder while the young lady wept.

Oh boy, Conrad thought. These were not easy times for anyone. He wished for a second they were still in high school, he and Lucinda and Glen and Paul and Mariella, who apparently had spent time in Uzbekistan. All these years she'd been wrapped in the tissue paper of his memory, safely seventeen. Was it possible that Mariella Cuore had really lived anywhere besides Clementskill? *No way*. She was such a pretty girl. Then he remembered more, her passion and grit. *Yes,* he corrected himself. *Of course.*

Chapter 8

*B*lind dates are supposed to be terrible.

Mariella reminded herself of this as she stood in a stall in the ladies room of the chicest, loudest, most crowded Italian restaurant in New London, Connecticut.

Blind dates make good stories, not good dates. It had been true when her mother was young, and it would be true when Mariella was a grandmother.

She needed to believe it, because this date was the worst. Her companion for the evening was named Leffert, for starters, and she couldn't say it without thinking that it sounded like French for passing gas. Really, if she even thought about saying his name, she had to bite back a rude giggle.

Then there was the fact that he only wanted to talk about the improbable history of steel mills and vineyards of the Greater Boston Area. He smelled strange too, as if he'd dipped his clothes in smelted iron and then rolled over bunches of grapes. That would explain the faded purple spots all over his clothes, although it was possible her eyes were just giving out on her. She had to work so hard at keeping them open.

Wanda, her roommate, teaching colleague, and fellow Clementskill High graduate, had arranged this atrocious date. She would be arriving soon with her own blind date set up by her spinster aunt. Leffert apparently went to the same church as Wanda. Why she thought Mariella would enjoy an evening with him was far beyond any sane person's comprehension, but Mariella knew that poor Leffert wasn't trying to be a smelly bore. She listened to his stories with as much polite attention as she could manage while they waited for Wanda and her fellow to appear.

"Leffert!" She heard Wanda's voice boom from the other side of the restaurant and turned to wave her frantically over while giving her tortured, imploring looks. When Wanda came closer, though, Mariella realized three important things. One, Wanda was wearing Mariella's lavender shirtwaist dress and her best white pashmina, which had been her grandmother's. Two, Wanda was looking at Leffert and Leffert was looking at Wanda, and they both looked mischievous and happy. Three, the young man in the Navy hat following Wanda took one look at Mariella, sat down next to her at the candlelit table, and held out a strong, warm hand.

"Hello," he said. His features were dashing, his eyes dark. "My name is Quincy Sellesbury, and I think this might not be a terrible blind date after all."

Mariella and Quincy had a rather quick romance; Quincy proposed in the summer of 1965 and Mariella said,

'Yes!' She got a taste of naval life while visiting Quincy at a base in Florida, and finally the couple settled in California when Quincy received orders to the USS Permit, a newly commissioned nuclear submarine stationed in San Diego. Not long after their first child was born, Quincy hung up his officer's hat for good and took a top-level civilian job in the field of strategic marine security.

Mariella loved being married. The few years she had lived as a single girl in the city, she had some fun, but mostly she read paperback romances in the ratty armchair in her small apartment. She loved waking up next to Quincy. She loved cooking for the two of them. She loved that he took care of all the bills and the gutters. He treated her with love and kindness, committing himself to their marriage with the utmost seriousness. Her mother said she would find the right man in God's time, and she did.

When her beautiful boys were old enough, Mariella went back to the classroom in California where she taught grades three to seven at various times. She was recognized as the outstanding teacher of the year by her local school district on more than one occasion and was regarded as one of the best. She had the reputation of being totally devoted to her students. For a brief time of five years Mariella taught the GATE (Gifted and Talented). On vacations, she and Quincy and the kids traveled to any place they could poke their finger on a map: Venice, Madrid, Jakarta. However, there was one special spot. Her grandparents had a lovely summer home in Northern New England on Hemlock Lake. Mariella spent her childhood at the lake, and she convinced Quincy of its quaintness. Finally, in 1992, she and Quincy were able to purchase a summer home on the lake from friends they had grown to love and admire. It was a very special time for the two of them, because this special place had been in Mariella's family decades ago, and now it was back in the family.

Mariella and Quincy and their boys enjoyed many summers there.

When Mariella retired from teaching after 30 plus years Quincy joined her, and they settled in North Carolina, not far from Quincy's best friend from the naval academy, Elliot, and his wife, Judy. Full of vim, chasing vigor, Quincy and Mariella pursued their hobbies and visited friends, loved up their grandkids and made plans for a long and fruitful stretch of senior years.

The brain cancer diagnosis shocked them. Quincy hadn't been feeling up to his usual snuff for a while, but who did? They weren't teenagers anymore. His decline was brutal, and it was fast. Before Mariella could draw a full breath he was a husk of the man he'd been, skin and bones held together with suffering, and then he was gone. Nine months after the news that her husband had cancer, a priest was intoning the hallowed old words over his grave.

Elliot and Judy didn't leave her side after she lost Quincy. His brother, Gerry, looked after her too, and her siblings loved her and watched over her. Even her treasured friends on the West Coast, Mitchell and Diane, called and wrote and visited as much as possible during that first year of grief. The time passed in a disturbing merry-go-round of blurred days, sweet memories, and moments spiked with aloneness so great she prayed in cries. She had not been alone for more than forty years. She didn't know if she could survive.

But she did. She hung on. A few years into her widowhood, her old friend Lucinda Barrett called her up and with two more high school friends, MaryJo Devons and Anne Kitts, they organized a reunion for four at Mariella's North Carolina house.

The visit was a balm to her soul; she told Elliot and Judy. The four women just clicked, as if no time had passed. Except of course all sorts of time had passed, and with it tragedies and triumphs, so they all had much more to talk about than boys and homework.

"Though we talked about boys and homework, too," said Mariella during her weekly phone call with Elliot and Judy. They'd spent an hour reviewing financial issues that Mariella needed to manage precisely, and they all were grateful for the change of subject. Elliot and Judy sensed lightness in Mariella's voice as she told stories from the weekend. It was beautiful to hear.

"We talked about Mr. Cormorand, who we called Mr. Cormorant because he did really look like a bird, and all his pens used to fall out of a hole in his front pocket that somehow he never knew was there; and no one ever told him, not even any of the teachers. I don't know why. That was just the way things were with the Cormorant."

She laughed. "Lucinda reminded me of the blue and yellow cheerleading uniforms. The skirts went down below our knees. And we wore long sleeves. They were pretty comfortable, though, and you could get a nice swish going with the skirt if you spun around just right."

"I didn't know you were a cheerleader," said Judy. "So was I."

Mariella and Judy traded cheerleading memories until Elliot broke in. "So who were the boys? You mentioned boys. Did they treat you like the number one queen you are? If not I'll happily go have a few words with them. Or break their legs, whatever you wish."

The image of kind, thoughtful, smart Elliot defending her teenage honor gave Mariella the giggles. He was very protective of her, though; she didn't doubt he would try if provoked.

"There was only one boy, and don't worry, he was a gentleman," Mariella said.

"What was his name?" Judy and Elliot asked at the same time.

"Conrad Holbrook."

Elliot harrumphed. "Sounds like something out of one of your romance novels, Judy."

"Oh hush, grumpy. I like it. Were you two serious?"

Mariella thought for a moment. "We liked each other very much. We did everything together, Math Club, acting, ice-skating and especially dances. We always had a lot to talk about." She sighed. "It was so long ago. We never came to an agreement, if that's what you mean. He went away to college and then I did. Well, I wrote a long silly sentimental letter after we broke up. It was just a special time in our lives. I wore his class ring! I forgot. I loved that ring. I loved him."

Judy sighed too. "Your high school sweetheart. Unforgettable, right?"

Mariella rubbed her knee, sore from the treadmill walking she'd started at Elliot's urging. "What about you, Judy, do you remember your high school sweetheart?"

"I should hope so," said Elliot. "She married him."

Mariella iced her knee and took a hot shower, not exactly the treatment her doctor had described, but oh well. She felt better, so live and let live, right? She was tired, with a little weepiness creeping in, as she often was after a long gab with Elliot and Judy. It was so nice to talk, but when she hung up the loneliness roared back like it resented her for forgetting it. She missed Quincy so terribly much. She thought about Franco, her last birthday gift from Quincy. Franco was so precious to her. He always gave her his unconditional love. She recalled that Quincy had wanted to surprise her with a trip of all places back to Clementskill where he had located a special yellow Lab puppy as a surprise birthday gift for her. Quincy was driving down the road to the kennel when Mariella had a flashback. She recognized the road as one of the back roads she and Conrad had frequented. Mariella kept the thought private as Quincy rounded the corner to the kennel.

Franco was a wonderfully special gift from Quincy, such a treasure and sweet memories.

To help her fall asleep for the three or four hours she might get in a row, Mariella replayed her favorite moments from her weekend with the high school 'girls.' MaryJo's stories from the big city paper. Anne's stories of her church choir. Lucinda's stories of all the high school chums she'd run into over the years.

Her mind drifted back further, to high school itself, and the brief blessed time she went steady with Conrad Holbrook. He must have become a remarkable man. *Whoever he ended up marrying,* she thought as she finally relaxed into sleep, *she is one lucky girl.*

Part Three

Chapter 9

A few weeks passed before Conrad skied again.

There were several days of December fog and unseasonable rain and slopes turned into slush marred with mud. He and Ben talked about driving north, all the way to Quebec if they had to, just to see real snow, but Ben couldn't get away from work, and Conrad didn't want to take the long trip on his own.

Besides, he stayed busy. He had always been a man in motion. Sammy, his clever, sturdy blue heeler-ish mutt, needed walking. The house needed small repairs. He also had his volunteer work as a sales and marketing consultant for local non-profits.

He visited with friends. He attended and relied upon church services. He talked with his children, and he biked and hiked, keeping his body strong for whenever the snow decided to fall.

And Christmas was almost here. One afternoon, he'd looked around the quiet house, bothered by something he couldn't pin down. The house was barren, but he was used to dodging the reminders of his loneliness. He worked so as not to notice how the shadows never seemed to leave the corners of the living room, or how the air above his wife's side of the bed seemed stuck in time, waiting for her to come back. He tried not to think about how he so rarely spoke aloud in the house that the sound of his own voice surprised him when he answered the phone. He didn't want to appear weak or ungrateful, foolishly ruled by emotion, so he didn't talk about the tumult that gave way to numbness in his heart. He didn't know how to talk about it, or about how hard, how beautiful and awful it was to shepherd Laura through the end of her life. The secrets hardened him, made him feel less than alive. He tried never to admit, even when he woke at three in the morning, that when the thought of next spring, next summer, five years from now crossed his mind, he could not see himself there.

But looking around the house that dreary December afternoon, he did see one undeniable thing. There weren't any Christmas decorations up. This he could fix.

Conrad rooted in the attic and garage for the boxes of garlands and bulbs, all the sweet and simple pretty things his family had gathered over 49 years. He felt his old energy surge into his arms and hands, the lifelong drive that always made Laura chide him to relax a little. She often tried to encourage him to slow down a bit and enjoy the scent of their summer roses on the breeze. He flipped open the top of the first box and dug in.

Three hours later, dusk deepening into night, he stood in the middle of the living room. Electric candles glowed on each windowsill. An ancient, hardy strand of popcorn and dried cranberries wound around a small, elegant sculpture of a Christmas tree that Laura bought in Austria. Christmas lights outlined the bay window, and small and large Santa Clauses, reindeer, and elves populated the side tables and mantle. Conrad had cut fresh balsam swags and had collected a tote bag of pinecones to accompany the decorations. The dark greens and browns mellowed the glitter and shine. It was simple. Conrad could tell it was good, and it felt like home.

Sammy barked at the front door. The driveway was nearly a quarter of a mile long, but he always caught the crunch of the postal-truck tires. Conrad placed an elf on the mantle before gathering up his coat and boots to make the trek to get the mail.

They walked together, Sammy sniffing at his usual spots and marking them with efficient authority, as a soft wind sent tremors through the brown beech leaves still clinging to the thinnest branches. The air felt fuller than usual. Conrad hadn't seen the moon since early November, but tonight he thought the light held some of that pearly glow, even through the low, convoluted clouds.

"Sammy," he called, as the dog began to bound after a squirrel or phantom in the Balsam trees that crowded the driveway. Sammy was a good dog, but he could be single-minded in pursuit. Last week, he'd circled the big grey birch in the front yard for an hour, convinced his vigilant attention would bring the chipmunk back down the trunk.

"Let it go Sam," Conrad said. His voice, rough from disuse, seemed to ride on the light wind, up and around the trees. "Let's just go get the mail."

Sammy trotted back to Conrad's side, and the two stepped and squelched among the puddles. I miss you,

Laura, Conrad thought. But I know you're safe, waiting for me on the other side. I'm okay tonight. I'm okay for now.

He opened the mailbox door and slid the pile of paper out. The AAA magazine, an offer to switch electricity providers, the local weekly paper, a phone bill, and a small, square envelope with 'Conrad Holbrook' written in a looping hand.

Conrad stared at his name.

He didn't know whether he wanted to laugh or weep. He turned the envelope over, and there it was, in that friendly, girlish cursive: Mariella Cuore Sellesbury.

He closed his eyes. "Thank you," he prayed. When he opened them again, it had begun to snow.

Chapter 10

December 23, 2012

Dear Mariella,

What a nice Christmas gift — your letter. I enjoyed reading it and am glad you decided to send it through the mail, as I never received it as an email. For someone who has gone through so much grief and loneliness, you have learned a lot and your words help. They are comforting. By the way, there are no boundaries between you and me. I welcome the opportunity to talk with you. I keep myself busy during the day...but the evenings are very lonely. It is so quiet around the house. No one to talk to, except Sammy, my dog.

I started reading the book, with a Bible verse for every day that you included with your letter. I am up to March already. Some are very poignant. Laura had family in Corinth, New York, and I always poked fun at her for the number of Gospels, or letters that Paul sent to the

Corinthians. March 18 makes you look at love and loss a little differently. Corinthians 13: "Faith, Hope and Love. But the greatest of these is love."

I would like to give you a call between the Holidays. From reading your letter, Mariella, I know I need to talk more with you. I have many friends, but every time I get near the subject of loss and loneliness, the conversation goes flat. It's because they all have their spouses and I can appreciate they just do not know how to respond. Others try to avoid the subject altogether. Feelings and emotions are not easy for me to talk about but it is becoming more apparent to me that they need to be brought out. You and I know each other well enough and we have a common thread in our lives. It is a wonderful coincidence after all these years that I came into contact with you again at a time when both of us are in need of a friend.

Send me your telephone number. I am looking forward to talking with you.

Don't hesitate. That's not good for either of us.

Merry Christmas, Conrad

December 24, 2012

Dear Conrad,

Your letter arrived at just the right time... I had been having a few down days, missing Quincy during this special time of year. But I will get to spend time with my son, Danny, soon, and that will be the answer to making this year's Christmas really special.

You'll be in my prayers this year. I'm sure your children and their families will take super care of their dad.

You mentioned the evenings... Yes, it is a very lonely time. My dog, Franco, is such a comfort. He seldom leaves my side and always has an opinion about what I'm doing. Sunday I made Italian wedding soup — a Christmas tradition in our house — and Franco was right beside me in the kitchen. We somehow do communicate with each other. Actually, right now it is close to his dinnertime and he is letting me know. What a pooch! I hope Sammy is a comfort and companion for you.

I had to chuckle when you said you had already read the book I sent through March. I did the same thing when I bought it! Corinthians 13... beautiful words. Love never ends, never. As I read it over again, I understood that the stronger your love was and is, the more strength you receive to be able to love more. This makes wonderful sense to me.

You are right about it being hard to share your feeling as one who has lost a spouse. My friends are so dear and loving, but they aren't "widows"! We do many things together, but I come home — "alone"! It is hard. I miss the hugs, the gentle caresses, the intimacy. At times it doesn't take much to set me off...tears can just begin to roll down my cheeks.

And you know what? That is okay.

Church is my heavenly place, but the music so often moves me to tears. A few weeks ago the choir sang "Eternal Father" — the Navy hymn. I lost it. Quincy was a Navy man. Even when he left the service, his work still kept him close to it. In writing this, I realize you don't know very much about him. I would love to know more about Laura. Feel free to share.

My phone number and email address are below. I look forward to talking with you. Again, thank you for your sweet letter.

Warmly, Mariella (and Prince Franco)

P.S. I totally agree that it's rather special connecting with you again.

Saturday, December 29, 3:22 p.m.

From: cholbrook

To: marcuor62

Subject: Sunday evening

Mariella,

Your letter brightened my day. I will call you tomorrow evening (Sunday) around 8 p.m. We have six inches of new snow tonight, so I'll be skiing (alpine) and then visiting with my children. Church services this evening first.

Looking forward to hearing your voice again, Mariella. Much to talk about!

Conrad

Saturday, December 29, 11:01 p.m.
From: marcuor62
To: cholbrook
Subject: Sunday evening

Hey Conrad,

What a nice surprise to see your email. Snow here, too, our first of the winter. How I love the snow. But I hope tomorrow it is okay to drive to church.

I shall look forward to our visit. It truly has been a very, very long time. Can you believe over 54 years? Where did the time go?

Chapter 11

*M*ariella picked up her book, "Team of Rivals." She put
it down. She went into the kitchen and brought her
Italian cookie press out of the cupboard. Maybe she would
make pizzelles for the next meeting of the Altar Guild.
That was ridiculous; the next meeting wasn't for two
weeks. She picked up Franco's food and water bowls and
put them in the sink to wash them, but left them there and
straightened the magnets on the fridge.

Franco barked. If she was handling the dishes, it was
perfectly reasonable for him to expect that they would
soon be filled with food, but Mariella had now moved to
the pots of herbs growing on the kitchen windowsill,
plucking withered leaves and switching the pot of basil

with the pot of oregano, then switching them back. Franco barked again.

Mariella reached down and patted his head, missing everything but the corner of one ear. Franco decided bolder action was in order. When Mariella crouched by the stove and took out all the pot lids stored in the bottom drawer, Franco ran behind her and nudged the hem of her sweater until his cold, wet nose touched her back.

Mariella shouted and leaped to her feet. She turned and looked at him crossly. He looked just as crossly back at her. She sighed. "Oh Franco, can you forgive your old girl?" She put his bowls back on the floor and opened the canister of treats. Franco deigned to accept three, then licked her index finger in a gesture of conciliation.

Mariella finally sat at the kitchen table. "I'm nervous, that's all there is to it. Fifty-four years. That's a long pause in a conversation, Franco dear. A long, long pause."

She straightened her shoulders. "Best keep busy. Nerves never did anyone any favors." She stood to fold a basket of clean dishcloths, and the phone rang.

Conrad's arms felt rubbery. The soles of his feet hurt. There was a stone in his throat. His stomach was going to explode, if his fingers didn't fall off first. He hadn't expected this; at 7:57, he felt fine. At 7:58, when he dialed Mariella's phone number, the laws of physics disappeared. He might as well have been seventeen again, asking out the pretty cheerleader with the shiny black hair and smooth white skin.

"Hello, Conrad." Her voice unfurled across the wires and the years. It curled up around his heart and rushed down his legs and into his arms, smoothing his forehead and lifting his shoulders, his ears, his chin. She knew it was him on the phone. She knew him.

"Hello, Mariella. Hello."

An hour and a half later, Mariella went to the kitchen, poured a glass of wine, and returned to her cozy chairwith Franco beside her. She kissed his muzzle. He curled up next to her, while she sat and sipped and thought until her knees began to ache. She and Conrad had made plans to talk again tomorrow night. At the end of the phone call, he'd said that he felt like they were just getting started, and she'd agreed. They were both shocked when each looked at the clock and saw they they'd talked for so long.

They stayed silent for a moment, not wanting to say goodbye. Mariella's ear was sweaty from pressing the phone to it; her neck had a crick and her mouth was dry. She didn't care.

"Is it very quiet in your house?" She could hear his breath, almost feel it in her ear.

"Yes," Conrad said. It had been easy to be cheerful with her, happy from his heart. They'd talked so much and with such quick familiarity he almost couldn't remember what they'd talked about. Her laugh was ringing in his ears like tiny bells, the way lilies of the valley would sound. "Sammy's sleeping at my feet, and he's snoring a little. I can hear the fridge, and the wood in the woodstove is crackling. But that's all. It's very quiet. It's nice. What about you?"

Mariella listened. "The furnace just came on. Franco makes a little whistle sometimes when he sleeps. I pretend he's dreaming he's Don Juan on the streets of Rome whistling at the pretty girls. He's very suave when he's in the right mood."

Conrad smiled. "I'd like to meet him."

"You're welcome any time," said Mariella. "We'd love to have you."

"I would love to come."

She blushed after thinking about what she had said while sitting in the chair, Franco whistling away, to think she had been so suggestive. Then she gave a little shrug. There was nothing wrong with letting a new friend know that you enjoyed his company. Even if the new friend was an old boyfriend who once held your hand every day walking to school, who once kissed you every night when he walked you home.

Conrad slept, and he woke, and there was no difference between the two, except Sammy changed sleeping spots around the room. He wasn't tired; he wasn't fighting off the specters of how life should have gone, how he shouldn't be alone, how this or that decision would have changed everything for the better. He opened his eyes; he saw her face, the girl under the Clementskill moon. He closed his eyes; he heard her voice, the voice from the past, this time from North Carolina. He didn't know how much time passed between the opening and closing. All he knew for certain was that he had a new secret, and this one made his heart pound. All he knew was

that tomorrow night, he would talk to Mariella again.

Chapter 12

Monday, December 31, 8:06 a.m.
From: marcuor62
To: cholbrook
Subject: You

Good Morning Conrad,

Visiting on the phone with you was such fun. You sound marvelous. You do have so many blessings in your life, and I know I have them also. Isn't it a strange time for the two of us? Wowowow... It is so nice to be ourselves, such fun, and so comfortable. The Lord does work in strange ways.

Life is quite short as we both know, so what is the expression? Seize the day. Go for it...my new 2013 motto. By the way, I slept quite well last night. Yeah team! Enjoy your day of skiing (are you going like you said?) on the brand new snow. Don't break anything!

I look forward to visiting with you once again...11:45 pm tonight.

Hugs, Mariella

Monday, December 31, 5:59 p.m.
From: marcuor62
To: cholbrook
Subject: You again

Wowowow, Conrad, you sent pictures! You do have a lovely home, and I am so impressed you put up Christmas things. The greens are such a nice touch. I also do decorate, though putting up lights is quite a challenge, pinching my poor fingers with the staple gun, etc. A few cuss words — I can't help it! But the neighbors have never complained...HOHOHOHO...

And your photo! You look pretty doggone good for an old man! Just teasing. Now the ball is in my court, but you have the advantage, because you know how to use the camera and send the photo! I must get my dear friend up the street to come on by. She's a love and will help me.

You mentioned wine last night. When we got off the phone, I opened a bottle of La Crema, a very nice Chardonnay, and just relaxed and thought very long and hard about our conversation. It was really special. A nice way to end 2012. And tonight is New Year's Eve, a new beginning. I like that.

I am going to heat up some of my Italian wedding soup now. It is quite tasty, and healthy!

Talk with you later.

Hugs, Mariella

"Is it the movies you like seeing, or the movie theater you like being in?"

Conrad smiled to hear Mariella hum a soft, low note as she considered the question, an admittedly silly question, but one he knew she'd enjoy answering. If they looked at their watches, they would see they'd been talking for almost three hours. Neither of them thought to look.

"I like the movie, of course. Why would you go to a movie you didn't want to see? I want to see Les Misérables — I saw it on Broadway and the music is awesome — so maybe if you ever visit we could see it together." She paused. Conrad felt his heart swell, his throat tighten, but before he could say what he'd been thinking since last night, she went on.

"But if I'm really honest, and I feel like I can be honest with you, Conrad, right?, then I have to say that just sitting in that dark theater, knowing that I'm about to see something fantastic, well, it makes the world disappear for an hour or two. When the movie's really good and the theater's really good, you forget that the clocks kept ticking while you were in there, and you can't believe it's dark or that you're hungry when you finally go outside. I like that a lot. I like being swept away like that a lot."

"You're right," Conrad said. "You are right."

"Well, naturally," Mariella teased. "Don't you remember? I almost always am."

Conrad was quiet.

"Are you there, Conrad? Do you feel okay? You aren't coming down with something are you? Did you remember to eat dinner?" Mariella felt a lurch of worry. Did she offend him? Was her joking too bossy? Did she sound like a silly idiot nattering on about the movies?

"You're right that we can be honest with each other," he said. "I feel I can be honest with you."

"I feel the same way," said Mariella. "I, well, I've been having a wonderful time." She grew shy. Conrad was so quiet, so suddenly. And yet his quietness felt warm, not like silence, not like he was hiding. She waited for him to speak.

"I love you, Mariella."

Rockets went off in her mind; sirens and gongs blared. *Conrad is in grief. Conrad is lonely. Conrad doesn't even know what I look like. He's just picturing a sixteen-year-old cheerleader in a velvet skirt to her knees. Conrad is crazy. This is crazy. I'm crazy. We are too old for love.*

"I love you, Mariella. I think part of me always has, deep in the back of my heart. I don't know how it's possible, but it is. I loved Laura. She was my wife, and we were happy together, really happy. And now, I love you, too. I have two loves in my heart, separate loves, and neither one makes the other one less. I don't know how this is possible, Mariella, but it is."

One thought flooded Mariella's body, up her legs and down her spine and across her chest. All she had to do was say it out loud in a very soft voice.

"I love you, too Conrad."

They could hear each other grinning. "This is a little crazy, isn't it?" Mariella just wanted to hear his voice again.

"Maybe," Conrad said. All the antic eagerness of the last 24 hours settled in his chest. He felt invincible. He felt lucky. He felt calm. "Is it hard to tell me you love me?" He just wanted to hear her say it again.

"Oh, darling, no. I love you. I always have. You were my first love, and I loved Quincy. That was a separate love, not the same. Oh, it's hard to explain. But Conrad, if it weren't true I couldn't say it. I love you."

Conrad wanted to touch her face. He wanted to see the woman she had become.

Sammy, alert to the emotion in Conrad's voice, walked over to him from the woodstove and put a stiff paw on his knee. Conrad rubbed his dog's head and then slid off the easy chair onto the hardwood floor in front of the stove to pull Sammy onto his lap and press his cheek against his white and grey fur. He was too full of love to stay still any more.

"Marry me, Mariella."

She thought of Conrad's closing words in his last letter to her:

Don't hesitate. That's not good for either of us. So she didn't hesitate one heartbeat more.

"Yes."

Chapter 13

Tuesday, January 1, 2:46 a.m.
From: cholbrook
To: lucinda_barrett
Subject: Happy New Year

Thank you!

Always in My Heart

Chapter 14

Tuesday, January 1, 3:37 a.m.
From: marcuor62
To: cholbrook
Subject: I am here, believe me

Dear, Dear Conrad,

I should be in bed asleep, but you, of course, have been on my mind. You must listen to what I have to say here, Conrad. I am very old-fashioned, and it's not like me to be forward, but this is important, more important than the wonderful words you said to me tonight. I am not sorry we spoke the truth of our hearts, though my head is spinning, but you must listen to me now, and you must believe me.

Conrad, you must give yourself room to be sad. Grief takes its own time. I know you don't like feeling that way but it is normal, and tears are normal. You do need time. You want to be able to skip over this, but no can do — you are a human being with so much love in your heart, so you need to heal. Let yourself do that.

I can be very patient. I shall be. If you let me I want to help you through this. And by the way, these feelings of sadness and grief have nothing to do with weakness in a man, so erase that from your thinking, please. This is what life is all about. We are going to continue to go through so many more challenges in our lives, and we can do that together. If you will let me help. You are and always have been so warm and so sensitive about so many things, and now you are grieving, so let go and take one step at a time.

Slow down, my love. Laura's death is hitting you hard, thus the tears in church or a memory. Give yourself time. You do have time, even though you are in a rush.

Slow down. I am not going anywhere. Talk to me, I hope every day, because I love hearing your voice, and it would be wonderful to see you, but if for some reason in the next few days you feel like, 'whoa, I need to slow down with Mariella,' I will understand.

This is not an easy time at all. We have made the connection, and my feelings can only get stronger (I don't know how that is possible, but it is), but we have time. So stop, take a deep breath. By the way, deep breathing exercises are excellent for making one feel so much better about things, and a great way to start the day.

I love you dearly. These words come from my heart. I do worry about you, Conrad. You are a human being, and you need time to heal.

Now I am heading to bed. I'm pooped! Many hugs, Mariella

She read her email twice before she sent it, and then again out loud. Part of her wanted to throw it in the trash and let Conrad sweep them both into a fever dream of rediscovered love that would crush the loneliness she had learned to endure. His ardor signaled escape, and some days, Mariella craved only an end to the constant weight of a widow's suffering.

But she didn't toss the letter or her better wisdom. Mariella knew grief, and she knew herself, and she had survived too much to trust easy endings. Happy endings she believed in, because lovers always had to work for those. There were no shortcuts to life. She needed Conrad to know this, too, and love her with a heart that was free to love.

And, oh, she wanted Conrad to love her. She had the sense to be abashed at the speed of their passionate declarations, but she wasn't sorry. She knew she wasn't wrong. She was a woman who tended to love, who felt right in herself when she had a man beside her, sharing the daily troubles and small pleasures. She liked arranging her mind around the presence and needs of a mate; she preferred it. She had never entirely understood her old friend MaryJo's decision not to marry, though she saw how much pleasure her work afforded her. Mariella would give up her house, the cars, the boat, even her teacher's pension (but never Franco) to rest in the arms of a loving companion again.

She clicked open the picture Conrad had sent her of himself. *He is handsome,* she thought. *He is kind. He is all that I thought he would become. He is my hidden treasure. He is my friend.*

The feeling in her chest was unfamiliar. She sat back in the office chair. Was she having a stroke? A heart attack? When was her next appointment with the cardiologist? It was as if a balloon were filling too fast inside her, stretching her ribs to their outermost limit.

She pressed her hand to her heart. She realized she was smiling. It wasn't pain lifting her up and out of her chair, across the room to the windows that looked out over the gray-blue sky. However long it took Conrad to come to peace with his grief, she believed he loved her. They would be each other's new and lasting home. The feeling was happiness.

"My Lord, my Lord, thank you," she said, her eyes shining to the sky.

"I looked at the calendar, and I can drive down to visit you in three weeks. That would be January 23."

Mariella laughed. "Conrad, you said you read my email but now I don't believe you! What happened to slowing down?"

Conrad petted Sammy's head. He'd taken to calling Mariella from the same spot on the living room floor, with his dog stretched out next to his left leg. It wasn't entirely comfortable to sit on the floor so long — they'd talked for four hours so far tonight — but it felt fun, and silly, and right.

"I did read it, and you're right. I know there's a lot I have to go through, but I want to be able to share it with you, and share your ups and downs. I want to be with you. And by the way, you were the one who invited me to see you." He saw no reason to wait. He felt no doubt in his heart.

Mariella was quiet. "But you're going to make me twiddle my thumbs for three whole weeks until I can kiss you?" she said at last, and blushed.

Conrad's stomach flipped and fizzed. "So I can come? You feel alright about it?"

"Yes," Mariella said. "But first thing, we're going to see Father Tim."

Conrad laughed at her this time. "I can't wait," he said. "We'll arrange a meeting with Father Tim and ask for his counsel. We might feel like teenagers, but we don't have to

act like them."

At that, Mariella threw all her caution to the wind.

Wednesday, January 2, 1:26 a.m.
From: cholbrook
To: marcuor62
Subject: Yes it is me

Dear Mariella,

We have said so much to each other. This is happening fast. I want to reassure you that I did read your email, and I have taken it to heart. I will always listen to you and respect your experience and perspective. But I think this is meant to happen, Mariella. I am thrilled! You have offered me something to look forward to. Time spent with you is happy time spent with a special person I really loved in the past — and you have reawakened those feelings. They are good feelings. I think we are so fortunate. I think this is God's plan for us.

I said some prayers for Quincy, also thanking him for taking such good care of you. I said my prayers, for Laura, though she is already in heaven waiting for me. I said some prayers of thanks to our good Lord for bringing you back into my life. If prayer and church service are

where you find peace and gain all your strength, I want to go there too...with you!

I have attached a video of me and my son, Ben, skiing on New Year's Day, like I told you I would. Going back to bed now. Just woke up thinking of you and wanted to send the video.

Good night. Love you.

Conrad

Wednesday, January 2, 4:29 a.m.
From: marcuor62
To: cholbrook
Subject: Re: Yes it is me

Good Morning...

Yes, I am up, I awoke at 3:15 with a smile on my face. So here I am. You make me so happy, you have no idea. Whoa! Franco is here beside me wondering what in the world is up...

I thanked God last night for sending me YOU. I thanked him for the miracle. And that is what it is. What a wonderful plan He had for us... That sounds unfeeling, and I don't mean it to, because losing Quincy was not my plan. Nor was losing Laura yours. But God is the one in control, so faith comes in and we have that. We just need to hold on to it.

I can hardly wait to hear your voice tonight. I think about you and your words and that just brings a wave of comfort over me... Wowowow... Never did I think I would feel like this again.

I am going to hold you in three weeks. Be prepared — I may never let you go. Please take care of yourself, be patient with yourself, prayer is going to help you so much. My priest gave me a book I can't wait to share with you, a study on the 62nd Psalm. Here is the beginning of it, as you know:

For God alone my soul in silence waits;

from him comes my salvation.

He alone is my rock and my salvation,

my fortress;

I shall never be shaken.

Conrad, the book is beautiful and wonderful for me. When I am in church early, which is most of the time, I read the psalm in the Book of Common Prayer.

I am so blessed...over the top...just crazy me with words popping out of my head! Best I do something constructive, now that it looks like I'm up for the day.

Love you lots, talk later, take some deep breaths,

Mariella

Wednesday, January 2, 7:05 a.m.
From: cholbrook
To: marcuor62
Subject: Re: Yes it is me

Good Morning,

11 hours sleep and I feel great. I'm at the non-profit today, running a workshop next week. Have a great day...get plenty of rest and I'll call you after 8 p.m. this eve.

Thinking of you a lot

Love you, Conrad

Wednesday, January 2, 5:19 p.m.
From: marcuor62
To: cholbrook
Subject: Re: Too long!

> Hey, I just walked in the door! I had a wonderful day. I can't stop smiling and singing. I really, really missed you, too. Amazing, we are on the same wavelength... Amazing. I can't eat or sleep. To lose a few pounds, that is good, but no sleep — not so good!

> Talk to you soon... love you lots.

> Mariella

Wednesday, January 2, 10:04 p.m.
From: marcuor62
To: cholbrook
Subject: I know that I just...

> ...got off the phone with you, but I wanted to tell you one more time — I dearly love you to pieces. Our talk of the wedding, the nights and days to come... Oh Conrad, you are my prince.

> Lots of hugs and wonderful dreams,

> Mariella

Thursday, January 3, 6:38 a.m.
From: cholbrook
To: marcuor62
Subject: Your prince

Up early after a good night's sleep. Of course the first thing to do is to read your nighttime wishes and thoughts for us and then to let you know before I start the day that you are the first thing on my mind and will be all day. If you were not here to fill my time with these wonderful thoughts, I would most likely be walking around with a rain cloud over my head. You have enabled me to experience sunshine and dreams of many happy days together.

The more I talk with you I am constantly amazed how closely we share the core values of our lives. We think alike in so many ways. I don't know if this is a result of sharing ourselves so deeply in our early adult lives, and that has carried through all the years, or if it is yet another piece of God's plan.

Have a wonderful day. I'll be thinking of you and looking forward to time with you this evening.

Love you,

Conrad

P.S. I am so glad you sent that letter, even though you'd written the email. It turned everything around for me. I treasured it. I am embarrassed to say, I have it memorized.

Chapter 15

C onrad set his briefcase on the floor of the conference room. He came to the Greenwich Center, a small business development non-profit, twice a month to lead marketing seminars and help owners create marketing plans. He'd made some good friends with the other presenters, and he found the enthusiasm and drive of the young owners inspiring and invigorating. During most of Laura's illness, and in the weeks after she'd passed, coming to Greenwich Center made him feel better, but still he felt as a molecule moving through the world. His students filed in, greeting him with kind hellos and questions. Conrad smiled. He tried to concentrate, and he heard his own voice telling a nervous and intent, couple who owned a specialty bakery, about the email newsletter tools they might use to reach their cake-loving customers. He even saw the couple laugh and relax at a joke he told, a joke he didn't even know he knew and couldn't remember after he told it. Mariella's voice, her warm and teasing manner, buffeted him like a chenille cloud. Through his introductory speech, his PowerPoint lecture, his acronyms and infographics, his anecdotes, his question-and-answer wrap-up, and his chatty goodbyes, he heard Mariella telling him stories about her dog, her treadmill, her church, her tutoring, and her Italian wedding soup. He heard her telling him she held him in her dreams. She felt so close to him, even in that fluorescent-lit conference room, that the tips of his fingers tingled.

"You seem happy today." Geraldine, a fellow consultant and longtime lunchtime pal, fell into step with him as they walked to the diner next door. "I haven't seen a group of small business owners look that enthralled at a marketing seminar in, well, ever. You were practically glowing."

Conrad smiled. Mariella! He thought and looked to the woman walking next to him. A part of him fully expected to see Mariella there, about to thread her arm through his, and when he saw tall, wry Geraldine instead, his fantastical morning shrunk like a punctured raft. He realized it was cold out, and he'd forgotten his wool hat in the conference room; he heard the growl of a squat snowplow clearing out the supermarket parking lot on the next block. The smell of the diner blanketed him, pancakes and fry grease, and his stomach sent up its first protest in days. Conrad was hungry. Had he eaten breakfast? Or dinner last night? Had he remembered to feed Sammy?

Embarrassment knotted his throat and flushed his cheeks, and his heart skittered as he fought to pack away the thought, the nearly real feeling of Mariella next to him. It would not do to go moony in front of Geraldine.

They found an empty booth and settled in. Conrad opened one of the laminated menus.

Geraldine stared at him. "Okay, enough. You've ordered the same grilled cheese sandwich on rye bread with half a pickle and an unsweetened ice tea for the last two years. You're not a menu guy. And are you blushing? What's going on? Are you in trouble?"

The concern in her eyes touched Conrad. She was a friend; he could talk to her. He could try. Besides, his efforts to act like Mariella didn't occupy his every thought were obviously failing.

"No, I'm fine," he said. He coughed. Geraldine raised an eyebrow. "I promise, Gerry, I'm fine. I'm great. I just, I might not be able to continue with the consulting."

"Conrad, you say you're fine, but you look like you've taken goofy pills. You're all red, you're coughing, and now you tell me you might not come back? Are you on a new medication?" Geraldine crossed her arms and sat back against the booth, now more annoyed than worried.

"I met someone," he said. Geraldine didn't move, except to drop her mouth a fraction of an inch. "On New Year's Eve."

She closed her mouth. "At a party?" She blinked, thinking fast, trying to make sense of this nub of a story.

"No, no, on the phone."

She threw up her hands. "Conrad! Those women are paid to act like that! You aren't in love, and your phone bill is going to be insane! You foolish man." She took a deep breath. "I'm sorry. I know you've been lonely — " She threw up her hands again. "No, I don't care how lonely you are." She dropped her voice to a hiss. "Phone sex is not the answer!"

Conrad looked bewildered, then hurt, shocked, and finally he started to laugh. He felt like a little kid in a fit of giggles. Giggles, at his age! They shook his belly and chest.

Geraldine was wrong, but she didn't lack for imagination, and he appreciated that. He pulled himself together as he saw her brow furrow and her eyes flash.

"It's not what you think," he gasped.

He inhaled and exhaled to banish the laughter from his voice. "On New Year's Eve, I spoke with a woman I haven't seen or talked to or even really thought about in more than 54 years, my high school sweetheart. We talked on the phone."

Geraldine propped her chin in her hand. A clever woman, a marketing consultant and lifelong business owner herself, she knew a meaty story when she heard one.

"We've talked every day since then," he said.

She raised her eyebrow again. "So you've talked three times since then, given that New Year's Eve was three days ago?"

"Yes," said Conrad. "And emailed several times. We plan on getting married, maybe in early summer."

Geraldine's mouth dropped a full inch. This was more worrisome than septuagenarian phone naughtiness. Conrad had lost his wife two months ago, and already he had turned his mind to marriage to a woman he loved when he was 18. Normally she would have launched into a full-scale attack on the perils of grief-induced romantic delusion, the disaster of impetuosity, and the impossibility of mistily-recalled teenage affection surviving elderly decay. She would have hacked at this threat to Conrad until it gave up and died. She had seen more than one friend lose his heart, and fortune, to the apparition of a late-blooming love — and it was almost always the men, the most accomplished men, who turned feckless and innocent after a lifetime of sturdy responsibility and emotional control. She'd watched these doomed affairs diminish their spirits. Their lives grew very small.

But she looked at Conrad for a long minute, not moving even when the waitress set down his grilled cheese and her Cobb salad. His face was relaxed. His eyes were bright and peaceful, and he appeared so intent and surprised, so much like a boy riding his first bike, that her sharp words softened. This might only be a dream for Conrad, and the eventual waking up cruel, but it wasn't hers to crush.

"That's awfully fast," she said quietly. She picked up her fork and stabbed a hardboiled egg with the force of her sublimated worry. "You're sure about this?"

Conrad nodded and spoke around a mouthful of grilled cheese. "I know it seems crazy. But there's something there, Gerry. It just didn't take long to see it. We think alike, we feel alike about so many things. I can talk to her, really talk. She makes me feel...happy. And, safe. I can talk with her about God and about losing Laura. She lost her husband three years ago, so she knows what it's like. She helps me understand. I didn't have to look for her. The love was just there."

Geraldine crunched through a piece of Romaine lettuce. "You know," she said at last. "Second marriages can be special. Happy! All the crap that gets in the way when you're younger isn't there. No work pressures, no little kids, not the same pressure on you to be this or that kind of grown-up. You're more grateful for the time you have left, so you enjoy each other more." She didn't trust herself to look Conrad in the eye, knowing the odds of the happy ending were long. She chanced a glance and saw him beam.

"Thank you, Gerry." He nodded. "You're the first person I've told."

They finished their lunch in a silence that was gentle, if not exactly easy. Geraldine wanted to shout at him, throttle him, get him to sign a pre-nup then and there, Google this woman's name and make sure she didn't have any convictions for fraud or axe-murdering or whatever it was widows were up to these days. A little part of her wanted to ask him why he didn't choose her to lift up his heart, if he was going to fall in love again so soon anyway, but she tucked this small loneliness away for tending later. She had no real interest in yoking her life to Conrad's; the longing for passion just never left a living soul completely, no matter how tough or old.

She pushed her salad bowl to the edge of the table. "So tell me about her, Conrad. What's her name? What does she look like?"

"Mariella Cuore Sellesbury." Geraldine made sure her eyes did not roll. Of course his lady had the most florid name this side of a Regency romance novel. Conrad didn't notice her grimace. "She was a year behind me in high school. She was a cheerleader."

"You went steady?"

"I gave her my ring," Conrad remembered.

Geraldine smiled. "Teddy Lawrence gave me his ring when we were seniors. I still have it. I kept it when we broke up. It looked better on me anyway. Did this Mariella keep your ring?"

Conrad threw a line deep into his memory. "No," he said at last. "She gave it back. I broke up with her, and she was hurt."

Geraldine allowed an eye roll. "You let the first love of your life go? Silly man."

Conrad nodded. "I was sort of stupid. I didn't really know what I was doing, just overwhelmed by everyone leaving and things changing, and my mother. She had some strong opinions, and I really respected her." He shrugged. "But when I met Laura, none of that mattered. It's like Laura moved into a different room in my heart."

Geraldine never spoke this intimately with Conrad. She hadn't thought he was capable of it. Even he seemed quietly delighted by his own words. This Mariella had changed him, opened him up, and it had only taken three days. "So what does she look like?"

Conrad flushed. "You mean when we were in high school?"

"No. We were all gorgeous when we were 17. We couldn't help it. I mean now, the, what, 69, 70-year-old woman whom you're going to marry?"

"I don't know," he said. "she hasn't sent a picture yet." He scratched his cheek. "But Ger, she's beautiful, I know it."

"What if she's got three arms? What if she has jaundice? What if she has tattoos? A lot of tattoos? Tattoos on her face?"

Conrad lifted his chin. "Then I suppose I'll get tattoos to match."

Geraldine inclined her head. "Alright, you romantic coot. You win. She sounds very special, and I'm thrilled for you." She reached forward and squeezed his hand. "I really am." She let go and leaned back. "And to prove it, I'm paying for lunch."

She left the bills on the table under the saltshaker, and the two friends shrugged their winter coats back on. They walked to the Greenwich Center, talking about their students and the tentative state of the economy, Geraldine's plans to invest in a solar tech start-up and Conrad's thoughts on town property values. Outside the conference room door, Geraldine stopped and pressed a hand to Conrad's elbow.

"You haven't told your children?"

Conrad pressed his lips together. He scratched his head and shifted his briefcase strap from one shoulder to the other. "I thought, maybe," he began. He avoided Geraldine's shrewd, understanding look. "No, not yet. I thought first..."

"You thought first what?"

He looked at her then. He blazed with hope. Geraldine was not a religious woman, but she silently prayed that all would be well for this gentle, determined man. "I thought

first I'd buy Mariella a ring."

Chapter 16

*A*re you talking about that Holbrook fellow, the one from high school?"

Elliot's voice boomed over the telephone. "Is he bothering you?"

Mariella walked back and forth in front of the fireplace in the living room. Franco, lying in his green corduroy bed, had long ago given up keeping track of her wanderings back and forth; now he just listened to the rise and fall of her voice and gave a small, affirmative bark every time she laughed. Which was every ten seconds during this phone call and the one before that, and all day, basically. Not that Franco minded. He was just fatigued from trying to keep up.

"Yes, it is that Holbrook fellow," Mariella laughed. Franco barked. "His name is Conrad, Elliot, Conrad Holbrook."

Judy broke in with her measured, loving concern. "So tell us again what happened, Mar. It seems like you must have left some part of the story out. You talked to him on New Year's Eve?"

Mariella told them the story for the third time. "And we've reconnected. It's very special. And I'm very happy."

Elliot and Judy were quiet. "What?" Mariella frowned. "You don't approve?"

Judy sighed. "Oh Mar, it's nothing like that. It's just a lot to take in. And, forgive me for being a nosey parker; it feels like there's something you're not telling us."

Mariella made another pass before the fireplace. "Well, we reconnected. I told you."

"Reconnected, reconnected, what does that mean?" Elliot said. "You built a bridge together? You plugged a phone in? What?"

Mariella's resolve wavered. She wanted to keep some of the preciousness of Conrad's love to herself, store it up to let the words and feelings caress her in the night until he could hold her himself. But this was Elliot and Judy. They deserved the truth, and they would be happy for her. She hoped.

"Well, Elliot, I want you to take two full, deep breaths before you say anything. Judy, make sure he does it." She stopped at her easy chair and perched on the edge. "Conrad and I are in love. He told me he loved me, and I said I loved him. We want to be together for all the time we have left."

She heard Elliot inhale sharply, exhale with force once, twice, then three and four times. She heard Judy cough, and then swallow a sound she couldn't identify. *Oh dear,* she thought. *Please don't disapprove. I am so happy.*

I am so happy.

"Hello? Hellooooo?" She tried to keep her voice light and jokey. Best not to let them know how scared she was of their reaction. "Earth to Elliot, earth to Judy! Anyone home?"

She heard little scuffles, little coughs, and finally the sound of Elliot blowing his nose. "Oh Mariella," Judy broke out, her voice catching on tears. "That's the most wonderful news."

Mariella started to cry with her friends. "It is, Judy, it is. He loves me. It's impossible, but it's true. We just knew. We just know."

Elliot cleared his throat. "Is he a good man, Mariella?"

She spoke quietly, her free hand clutching the arm rest. "Yes, he is."

"Then I am so happy for you," Elliot said. "It's crazy — don't let this silly crying fool you — I think what's happening is insane, but you've been lonely a long time. You and that big heart of yours! If you feel he's the right man for you, then we'll trust that he is. You deserve to be happy."

Mariella sniffled. "Oh Elliot."

"Are you crying?" Judy sniffled too. "Are we all crying?"

"I'm just so happy," Mariella sobbed. "And so tired. We've been talking for hours every night."

"A couple of teenagers, you are," Elliot blew his nose one more time.

"I cry when I'm happy and tired," Mariella said. "That's just who I am. And to know that you two support me is such a blessing."

She broke down, and Judy murmured soft encouragements until her breathing settled. "I haven't sent him a picture yet," she said. Panic brought more tears to her eyes. "What if he thinks I'm hideous?"

Elliot laughed at her then, and Judy joined him. "You're a foxy lady, Mariella," Judy said. "He's going to flip when he sees you. And forgive me, but none of us is what you'd call glamorous at this stage of the game. If he's the man you say he is, then he will love you all the more when he sees your picture, even if your hair is sticking up or you're sticking out your tongue."

Elliot's voice turned grim. "But don't do the last one," he said.

"It's suggestive."

That set Mariella off into laughter this time.

"But one thing, seriously," Elliot cut across the last of her giggles, and Mariella sat very still. "I don't want to be presumptuous, but if at some point you should need someone to walk you down the aisle, I'm definitely available. Just don't choose a date when we're on a cruise or something."

Mariella ducked her head. Elliot had guessed the truth, but it was too soon to share it all. She would wait until Conrad visited, until he proposed holding her hand. The old, proper ways of doing these things were still the best, even in such unexpected circumstances.

"Oh you goose," she said. "Take a deep breath! We're going one day at a time." She stood and walked to the fireplace, holding a palm out to absorb the mellow heat. "I couldn't have survived this last three years without you and Judy," she said. "I'm just grateful to have made it here.

"You would have made it one way or another," Elliot said. "You're stronger than you know. Let me tell you one more thing, though, so Judy can accuse me of bossing you around."

"You always boss me around," Mariella teased. "I'm used to it."

"Just remember that you are number one in this whole deal, right?" Elliot grew serious and intense. "Whatever is best for you, that's the best thing to do. You are a queen, and you ought to be treated as such. I never want to see you putting yourself second to please someone else. You come first, okay?"

Mariella nodded until she could speak through her tears. "Yes, Elliot. Thank you. I'll do what's best for me."

Judy sensed they'd all had enough emotion for one night. "As for Franco," she said, "he's actually number one, and he's not going to let you forget it." Mariella laughed. Franco lifted up his weary head, gazed at his suddenly effervescent friend, and barked, before giving in to a well-earned nap.

Thursday, January 3, 4:58 p.m.
From: cholbrook
To: marcuor62
Subject: Photo

> You are still gorgeous, Mariella! I always thought you were a beautiful lady. Your smile is still the same. You look radiant. And on the phone the Mariella I knew and loved 54 years ago comes across in the way you talk, your excitement, and your beautiful soft loving tender words. Thank you for sharing this photo with me.
>
> Call me after 8 p.m.
>
> Conrad

Friday, January 4, 12:37 a.m.
From: marcuor62
To: cholbrook
Subject: Goofy me

Golly I love you...

Do you realize we talked for over four hours and I did not want to let you go?

I had so much fun tonight. You make me laugh and giggle. You are such a dear. I was thinking about our old memories, but I get so excited when I think about all the new ones we will make together. What will we share? Where will we travel? I can't think of anything we won't enjoy, and if I can't go skiing always with you, I will love curling up by the fire just waiting for you to return. As long as you keep your eyes on the slopes, HOHOHOHO... no pretty women... NONONONO.

I love how we can laugh together and tease each other. I like you, and I love you. Wowowow. That is a wonderful gift. I feel so special right now in God's eyes. It is an amazing feeling.

On that note, best I get some shut-eye. I have an Italian meal to cook for my neighbor whose mother is quite ill. I've wanted to do this for days, but truly just couldn't focus at all...wonder why...

I love you with all my heart.

Mariella

Saturday, January 5, 10:55 p.m.
From: cholbrook
To: marcuor62
Subject: I love you

Just a wonderful evening talking with you tonight. My mind is filled with brightness now, and hope, and wonderful thoughts of you. I remember how easy it was for us to talk about any subject with complete freedom, and that is a gift you have, to be able to coach that out of me. This is unique to us and is putting even more depth to my feelings for you. This is where true love is located. You fill my thoughts. I dream of our cozy pajama get-togethers (your idea!), and the fire of my dreams warms my heart.

I can't believe I found that letter you wrote to me 54 years ago. It was pressed into the back page of my yearbook with the same paperclip you must have used. What a coincidence that I still had the yearbook with me, that it was exactly where I thought it was, in a box I took from my parents' house many years ago, that I hadn't opened it in all those years and that I found it just three minutes before we talked so that we could read it together.

You have an unbelievable gift to express heartfelt emotion that just wraps me all up in the meaning of love.

I love you dearly now as I did 54 years ago. What a romance movie this would make!

I am still wrapped up in all your hugs!

I love you for all that you have been and are in my life.

Conrad

Chapter 17

onrad read the letter out loud, all ten pages of it. Mariella could remember the words rolling out from her blue pen in her old room in the Clementskill house, crying over the pages and trying to keep her tears from blotching the ink.

"I sure was nuts about you, wasn't I." Mariella closed her eyes. The words from her heartfelt letter had left her memory a very long time ago; and yet they were precise, down to the feel of the sun on her arms in her room and the way he held that new yearbook against his hips while they stood with Lucinda and Paul on the school's front steps. The memories were like etchings, pressed between layers of vellum, illustrating in fine, angled lines an impossibly distant life.

"You had a big heart," Conrad said. He was amazed that she had loved him so intensely. How had he forgotten? It loomed inside him now, her devotion to him, and his smitten awe for her. "You were so easy and comfortable to be around. I wanted to be around you all the time."

"Didn't we have the best time? Do you remember your birthday party?"

"That party! You threw me a party! No one besides my mother when I was six threw me a surprise party. Danny Flanders sprained his wrist trying to knock down the piñata. I remember that," Conrad said. "And you made Italian wedding soup. And cake."

"And we danced to the Everly Brothers. You were such a good dancer." Mariella sang a line of the old, slow song.

"*Whenever I want you all I have to do is dream.* Do you remember?"

Conrad pictured her in his arms. She was smaller than he was. Her black hair had brushed against his jaw and chin, and his hand had pressed the middle of her back, pulling her as close to him as he dared. "I loved you very much, Mariella. The way you felt things so strongly, and could say them, it was amazing. It was your gift from God. Paul knew I loved you. He knew me better than I did."

Mariella smiled at the wistfulness in his voice. "Lucinda knew me better than I knew myself, too. She tried to warn me that going to college would be hard on us. But I didn't listen."

"I haven't told my children about us yet." Conrad rubbed his eyes with his hand. "But I want them to know that their dad is going to be with a wonderful woman for the rest of his life. I know they'll be happy for me. Next time they come, I'm going to show them this letter from

1959, so they'll see how much you love me and how beautiful you are."

Mariella wished she were next to Conrad, able to hold him and look into his eyes to weigh the balance of hope and grief that still moved in him without his full awareness. "Darling, I'm sure they will be happy for you. I hope so. But you have to remember, our reconnecting is probably not the story they'd write for you so soon after their mother's passing. They have no idea that I exist, let alone that we're in love. You and Laura had been married awhile before they were born, and then they knew you as their dad, not as a man in love. They might not recognize you as a romantic person, a passionate person. They love you and want to protect you, and I might seem like a threat to their precious dad. To their family. To their own hearts." She waited for him to disagree, but all was quiet. She took a deep breath and kept on. "I know I'm being forward, forgive me. But your children come first, and they might need time to accept this change in your life, as special as we know it is. We have time, my love. We have time to share our love."

Conrad whispered. "I want to hold you now, Mariella. I don't want to wait."

She thrilled to his words. "Conrad," she said, shaking her head. This was important. She wanted to meet and match his urgency, to give voice to the desire she thought she'd never feel again, but she wouldn't do anything to hurt his children; she had been thinking deeply about how to share her marvelous news with her own sons. "Do you hear what I'm saying? We know that we'll love each other forever, but they will need more time to believe you."

Conrad flipped through the pages of the letter again. "I hear you. I do. I don't know why, but this reminds me of when you told me not to rat out Margaret when she rooted through my sock drawer and found all the letters you wrote me when you were away during the summer."

"Your sister was full of spirit," Mariella said. "She was just trying to figure out who you were and who she was and how to grow up. I missed her company when you and I broke up."

"Never again," he said. "I'm not making that mistake again, not after God has given us to each other with all the love from 54 years ago. And I want more. I want to be with you now. I want to feel the love of your beautiful kiss."

"You're not so bad at expressing emotions yourself." Mariella said lightly. She closed her eyes, let her worries go. "Two weeks. Just two weeks. And then we'll sit by the fireplace, I have lots of pillows; we'll have a little wine, some cheese, but not too much sodium, and a fire, and you. You holding me tightly in your arms."

"Like I did when we used to dance," Conrad said. He reached into his cardigan pocket and closed his hand around the small velvet box he'd been carrying with him all day. He'd tell his kids about Mariella. He would tell them soon.

Their conversations grew longer, their emails more frequent. Mariella planned a trip for the first part of February. She scheduled a meeting with Father Tim. She floated through lunches and tea dates with friends, sharing the delicious news each time. She cuddled Franco, vacuumed the house, looked in after neighbors, slept poorly some days and well others, and smiled the whole time. She watched the skiing videos Conrad sent her — Oh, he was a speed demon! — and visited the websites he sent her on ice skating rinks they could go to near his house. She went to church and prayed through her happiness and through her tears, the two so close she didn't bother to separate them. She sent him pictures of Franco and of her kids and of the children she taught. She sent him the emailed congratulations and well-wishes from friends. She told him about her sore knee and her love-hate relationship with the treadmill and the pieces she played on the piano. She told him about the nightmares that startled her from sleep sometimes. She wrote to him about her daydreams of cooking together in her kitchen, of kisses, of his gorgeous blue eyes, of snowball fights and quiet mornings. She chided him to eat bigger breakfasts and to give Sammy hugs from her. She printed out her favorite letters and carried them with her, folded in her pocket like a magic trick, until she could see him again.

Monday, January 14, 7:49 a.m.
From: cholbrook
To: marcuor62
Subject: You

> Oh how loved you make me feel. It is such a wonderful feeling. Hard for me to admit, but maybe I am a romantic. I cannot say enough about the feelings I have for you, Mariella. They are genuine, they are deep, they are always there, they are warm, they are all wrapped up in the word Love. My days are now so happy, I am anxious with expectations. I am anxious for your physical presence in my life. I am anxious for

you as I start to go down this last glorious path in our lives. I am ready to relax for the first time in my life. That is all I wish to do. Relax, always with you beside me. You have made my day, you have made my life come together again, you have given me purpose, and you have given me a feeling of youth, a feeling of ompanionship. You are wonderful. You are what God has given me. You are such a loving person. You are a wonderful blessing to me.

I love you deeply. Conrad

Monday, January 14, 9:19 a.m.
From: marcuor62
To: cholbrook
Subject: You have my heart

Well, first you made me cry, for a little while, then you made me smile, then I began to feel warm all over. I took a deep breath and let it out slowly. I felt like you were right here beside me. It was such a special and unique sense of peace and happiness, a spiritual awareness that I am going to be okay. Talk about a gift from God...

Sometimes it is so hard for me to understand why I can be so fortunate. What have I done to deserve to have you back in my life? But I have also come to the realization — who am I to question God's plan? He is the wise one, and trust me, I want to go down this path with you for the rest of our lives.

Please remind me when you come to church, we need to light candles for Quincy and Laura. I don't want to forget that. Our comfort is their peace with God. Perhaps their comfort is to know we are happy and will be happy.

Okay, I need to get my act together and do something constructive for the rest of the day. I did have a super breakfast (I decided best I practice what I preach) and now to the treadmill. I can hardly wait...

The tears of joy have stopped, and now I can't wait to hear your voice tonight. Hugs hugs hugs, Mariella

Tuesday, January 15, 7:44 a.m.
From: cholbrook
To: marcuor62
Subject: Re: You have my heart

What a wonderful evening. I did not want to get off the phone. Your laughs and giggles excite me. Your voice is a melody in my ear. Your teasing is a joy to my heart, it tugs and tugs until you find the spot you are looking for to cozy up and stay. How fortunate I am! You warm my heart, you have refreshed my spiritual life, you have placed a permanent smile on my face. You have given me your love. I promise you, Mariella, with all the sincerity I can muster, I will take good care of this treasure, I will not ever discard it. If I can make you happy, I will be happy in return. My love for you grows deeper every evening I spend with you. You are an amazing woman.

I love you so deeply, so much...

You just make me happy!

Conrad

Tuesday, January 15, 10:00 p.m.
From: marcuor62
To: cholbrook
Subject: Three more days

Goodnight, Conrad... Thank you for being who you are. I am so thankful now that I have you for whatever time is left for us...

You waited a month for a letter from me, and now our wait is only three days. We can do this. It's just hard! I am just bursting with love for you and I want to express it — be ready! How's that for being outspoken? I know, shocking! I can't help it. But I will try to be patient, not forward or pushy, my emotions just get away from me, I am just so totally in love with you.

Thank you for the flowers and the card and words of love. Thank you for having the courage to write those six words in your first letter, "No boundaries between us" and "Don't hesitate." Those wonderful words changed our lives forever.1

I am picturing you in the newly fallen snow. How I wish I were there, just the two of us standing outside while the white, fluffy flakes spinwheel down, so quiet and peaceful and lovely. I would love the silence, and we would be in each other's arms. Now THAT is romantic!

You are truly loved by this woman.

Mariella

Chapter 18

onrad read Mariella's latest letter one more time before folding it into a tight square that fit in his down vest pocket. Outside, snowshoeing with Sammy on trails no one else had touched, his mind felt clear and powerful. He trusted his heart — he loved Mariella — but as his trip to see her approached, his practical self raised a stern hand. He was not an impulsive man. He'd never described himself as really emotional. Energetic, hard- working, not afraid of risk, dedicated to those he loved, full of faith, curious and intelligent — all those, yes, but heedless? No.

And yet Geraldine thought he was being foolish; he could tell. The young lady at the jewelry store had certainly thought so, the way she whipped around with her chin resting on her chest staring at him when he said he was buying a diamond ring for a woman he hadn't seen in 54 years.

So he prayed, and he thought it over, in the moments when he wasn't dreaming of Mariella or making plans to take her zip lining or canoeing or any of the thousand things she'd never done (and she was after him to try a massage). How could his love be possible? How could it feel so right? How could all this flowering romance, this effulgent joy, be coming from him?

He composed a letter in his head as he tromped through the crisp snow and brisk air, pretending he was writing to Mariella. These last two weeks, each time he wrote to her, his thoughts had come more fluidly, more daringly than ever before. Maybe this way he could explain himself to himself.

My Mariella: Isn't love supposed to be on one plain? Isn't love for one individual similar to love for another? But I see there is so much more possible than I thought. One love doesn't take away from another. Somehow the heart makes room.

We showed ourselves to be good people by the way we conducted ourselves and committed ourselves and loved our spouses in our previous 43 and 49 years of marriage. That set us up for a life of understanding, appreciation, affection, and joy for each other. I cannot ask for any more than what has been offered. I am so grateful to God for the blessing he has bestowed on you and me.

How fortunate, you still held those tender feelings for me and allowed them to mature into this romance we could only have dreamed of. How fortunate, I still held those tender feelings and encouraged them to come alive, blew on them to see if we could turn the embers into a glow again.

I love you with my whole being. Apparently I have always loved you but it was tucked away for safekeeping, for another time.

That time is now.

Just before the snowshoe trail looped up a small hill toward the house, Conrad stopped, peeled off his gloves, and unfolded Mariella's letter again. He read it through, reaching to hear her voice in the words, imagining what it would feel like to touch her again. Everything about this love felt right; it might be surprising, shocking even, to those who knew him as the reserved man he'd long been, but nothing about it was wrong.

"Two more days, Sammy, just two days!" He returned the letter to its pocket and scooped up a snowball for Sammy to catch. The dog always leaped up in a vertical line, his jaws snapping down on the soft ice that splattered his wet black nose and mottled fur. He landed on all fours with a bright, demanding look, his black ears pointing up, giving him the aspect of a curious, gentle wolf, certain that he would catch the snowball this time.

It startled Conrad, the perfect image of Sammy there. The dog had a corona of snow crystals around his muzzle, and his left front leg, lifted and bent loosely at the knee, quivered. Conrad had made arrangements to board Sammy at the local kennel the day after he proposed this trip to Mariella. Sammy had stayed there before, lying dully but not unhappily in the corner of his chain link room with an old rope chew toy from his puppy days. Conrad and Laura went on long vacations or consulting gigs. Neither dog nor man liked the separation, but neither worried about it. The man would come back, and the dog would greet him. They'd go about their business of walks and food, head scratching and snowball toss.

But this time, Sammy couldn't know that Conrad was leaving to see Mariella. His dog brain, clever as it was, couldn't predict that life was about to change, and Conrad was headed into territory, emotional and literal, that was thrilling — and unknown. Conrad felt all the heat flood out of his body at the thought that in a small but important way, he was leaving Sammy behind.

He started to cry. Sammy sat, then lay down and rested his head on his front paws. "Oh Sammy," Conrad said. "Come here, come here." Sammy trotted through the snow until he could press his body against Conrad, who knelt and wrapped his arms around his dog's neck. Sammy waited, his ears swiveling at the sound of a squirrel's nearby scamper. Conrad's knees grew wet and cold. The light drained out of the air, replaced by a quiet, smoky dusk. Conrad cried and cried.

"Oh Laura," he whispered. He let Sammy go but kept a hand on the dog's warm back as he found his thoughts turning to prayer. His bliss seemed to him simply the twin of his sorrow; the two held hands in his heart. "Oh Laura," he sighed. "I am happy. For whatever time I have left, I am happy. I pray that makes you happy too."

He stood, suddenly starving. Sammy jumped into a run, and the two friends chugged and hopped the final stretch of trail. At the house, they shared leftover rib-eye steak, mashed potatoes and half of an apple pie Conrad had bought two days earlier at a church bake sale. He grinned when he thought of how pleased Mariella would be at this big meal. She was always after him to eat enough to fuel his energetic ways.

He left the dishes on the table and went out to ready the car for the drive. Thorough and quick, he cleaned out the minor detritus of old umbrellas and coffee cups, checked the jack and spare tire, and repacked the emergency kit that he kept under the passenger seat. He filled a sturdy bag with sand from the bin by the garage and hefted it into the trunk along with a large snow scraper, a small red shovel, and an extra blanket and flashlight. He placed the road map with the highlighted route on the dashboard, and made sure the phone charger was in the glove compartment.

In the house, he packed a small bag with clothes and a book on faith he wanted to share with Mariella. He packed his toiletries and his laptop. In the front pocket of the suitcase, he slid the special card he'd bought for her, roses twining on the front and a love poem inside. He would leave it on her pillow, he thought, maybe when she was brushing her teeth. She would be so pleased. Maybe she'd already received the card with the bouquet of roses he sent earlier in the week.

When all the preparations were done and Sammy lay in his dog bed snoring, when Conrad had changed into clean, dry clothes and put on his warm leather slippers (he wouldn't remember to do the dinner dishes until after he returned from his trip), he sat in his spot on the living room floor. Soon he would call Mariella for their cherished evening talk.

First, though, he had to call his children. Such beautiful people, such good people, who had shown kind, constant care to him through these last few months even with all the demands of their own lives. No matter the cartwheels of his heart right now, his three children were and always would be his world. He knew they would be happy for their dad to be so happy. They would want to be brought into the circle of magnificent love he and Mariella had created, he knew. He hoped. He prayed. So, one by one, he called his children to tell them that he'd reconnected with a woman named Mariella, that he'd fallen in love, and that in two days he would be driving 1,000 miles to see her for the first time in 54 years.

"Two days!"

Judy covered her mouth with her hand. "Mar, that's soon! That's two days! He's really coming so soon?"

Mariella nodded. The two of them were wrist-deep in cookie batter, enough to make four dozen pizzelles as gifts for the kids Mariella tutored. Flour even dusted Franco's nose.

"I've vacuumed all the upstairs and cleaned both bathrooms," she said, wiping her brow and leaving a narrow streak of batter. "But there's still downstairs and this kitchen."

Judy shook her head. "Why don't you hire a girl to help you out? You said your knee's bothering you."

Mariella gave her bowl a quick, expert stir. "I know I should. But, this is special. I'm getting my house ready for Conrad. I want him to feel like he's coming home. Like it's his home."

They worked in silence, stirring, pouring dollops of batter into the hot pizzelle press, flipping the finished cookies onto a plate and dusting them with powdered sugar. Mariella hummed old pop songs under her breath. Judy watched her out of the corner of her eye. She doesn't know she's singing, Judy realized, and she marveled at the happy radiance of her friend. She had been in such pain for so long. This was the real Mariella, confident and jazzy, even moving around the kitchen differently, with a fluidity and kick Judy hadn't seen in years. It wasn't just happiness, Judy saw. Mariella looked sexy.

"So." Judy scraped the last of the batter out of her bowl. "So.what about the linens?"

"What about them?" Mariella broke a pizzelle in half and took a bite.

"Are you going to put fresh linens on the guest bed or just yours?"

Mariella coughed on her cookie. "Judy! Wowowow, that's a question and a half!"

Judy laughed and placed the bowl in the dish rack. "I'm sorry, Mar. It's a little awkward to bring it up, though it shouldn't be at this age. We're not teenagers tiptoeing around the boys so that we'll stay good girls. What could shock us now? And it's none of my business, really, but if you want to talk about it, I'm happy to listen. It's a big deal."

The women sat down at the kitchen table, each with a cup of tea and small pile of pizzelles in front of them. Both wanted to lose six more pounds, but they also knew better than to waste time worrying about weight when they had snacks and each other's company.

"It's so strange, Judy. Wonderful, amazing, to feel this way." She took a sip of tea. "To want someone." She took another sip of tea. "Physically." She coughed, then rolled her eyes. "Cover your ears, Franco," she called to the dog napping under the table. "This isn't fit conversation for royalty."

Judy smiled at her friend, waiting for her to continue. "It's strange to even talk about it," Mariella said. "It's like the body becomes a job to take care of, or put up with, or try to be grateful for, because it works pretty well. But not something to, I don't know." She looked frustrated.

"Enjoy?"

Mariella brightened. "Yes. Not something to enjoy. But I'm crazy about this man every way you can think of."

Judy was quiet. "What," Mariella said. Her face dropped, and she clutched her tea cup. "I thought you and Elliot approved."

"Well, first of all, you are a brave, smart woman, and you've become independent since Quincy died," Judy said. "You don't need us to approve of your choices."

"Elliot might disagree," Mariella said.

Judy conceded the point with a nod. "The thing I keep wondering about is what happens when you two see each other again, not as the teenagers you were and not as a photo but face-to-face, with these bodies. He's a voice on the phone and a lot of nice emails, but he's a real person, too. What if the voice and the letters don't match the man?"

Mariella sighed. "Or the same way for me, I mean for him. What if he's in love with a picture of me he's made up in his head, and he's in love with her, like a fantasy? Or if I'm doing that about him? I think about it. A lot. We might be seniors but we can still fool ourselves about love."

The women munched cookies in thoughtful silence. "So what do you come to when you think about it?"

Mariella looked away from the table, out the picture window over the sink. The flowering dogwood in the backyard was most certainly not flowering now; it looked fussy and too thin, like it was on a hunger strike to protest the closing of an Ann Taylor store. Come March, though, that tree would be the bride of spring.

"I think God is taking care of us," she said slowly. "I think, I remember what puppy love felt like. It was different from this. I can talk to Conrad. He can talk to me. I love how he makes me feel, but I love who he is, too. It's not just the idea of each other we want."

She smiled self-consciously and looked at Judy. "Mostly I think I don't know, but I love him. I believe he loves and wants me. And that makes me feel so excited and so peaceful, there's nothing I can do but trust that it's right. Trust in God. Faith, hope, and love. And the greatest of these is love."

Judy reached out and held Mariella's hand. "Passion is wonderful, isn't it?"

Mariella nodded, a little teary, overcome with gratitude for her good friend. "It's absolutely wild. I feel like I'm on one of Conrad's ski rides. He sends me videos. He goes so fast! My biggest worry is what a mess I'll be if I don't get enough sleep while he's here."

They gathered their plates and cups into the sink and began wrapping the cookies into gift bundles.

"I guess that answers my question," Judy said, winking.

"Judy!" Mariella scolded, turning her back to hide her sudden, enormous grin.

Thursday, January 17, 11.36 a.m.
From: elliotandjudy
To: marcuor62
Subject: The beautiful gift you've been given

Dearest Mariella,

I guess tomorrow is the BIG day and I hope with all my heart it lives up to all your (giddy?) expectations, and is the beginning of another beautiful chapter in your life. You are the best and from what I gather, so is Conrad, and we are as excited as you about what lies ahead.

BUT (enter the serious "Dad" countenance), Judy told me the bare bones of your recent conversation and I want to add my two cents. I'm only bossy because we love you! This is a moment to be true to yourself and remember you're the No. 1 until you choose to devote your energy and adoration to another worthy human being! Go slow, let the physical presence blossom at a rhapsodic pace, be coquettish but inviting, warm but tantalizingly at arms length, and let your happiness glow through it all. Fifty years is a long time and the memory and the physical reality, of an evolved personality with habits, quirks, mannerisms, even the occasional foul odor!, must realign in your heart and consciousness as the wonderful but changed person you willingly accept into your heart. Be mindful too that Conrad will be going through the same reconciliation of memories versus physical reality. I might sound old-fashioned, but don't be pushy, as guys don't generally like that in the formative stages of getting acquainted. But do let your independent spirit and newfound self-reliance shine through!

I'm rooting for this happy ending, but I'm also feeling protective of the beautiful fragile flower that you are, so deserving of joy without heartache. Judy says I'm being patronizing now, so let me end with--have a wonderful day and as many more days like it as a lifetime can bring!

Let us hear from you whenever and however you care to share.

Fondest regards,

Elliot

Chapter 19

W indy day, sunny and bright. Blue sky. He wakes up and emails her before he eats breakfast. *Leaving in an hour.* She wakes and writes back. *When you read this you will be here. How about that?* She vacuums the living room again. He counts the toll money in his wallet for the third time. He drops his dog off at the kennel with a long scratch around the ears. She drives her dog crazy with incessant, anxious hugs and kisses.

A thrum in her belly moves her around the house, secreting love notes behind cushions. A drumming pulse in his heart moves him down the highway on wheels that don't seem to touch the road. Seventeen more hours, he thinks. Seventeen more hours, she sings to her dog. Tomorrow I see my love. Tomorrow I hold my love.

Before he left, Conrad receives a phone call from his daughter, Suzanne.

She says, "So Dad, does she have a last name? What state does she live in? Does she have a home? A phone? Just wondering in case something happens along the way."

In his eagerness to see Mariella, Conrad had forgotten to include his children in on his itinerary. He makes the trip in two days, all 1,000 miles. He wants to drive down to meet her rather than meet her in an airport as he had not seen her in 54 years and would probably not recognize her. By driving he thought he would be able to meet Mariella in the privacy of her driveway.

Suddenly he is there, rounding the corner onto the street where she lived. He counts the mailboxes, and his heart starts to pound ever so loudly. Three more mail boxes, two then, there is the house. This woman he loved, this woman he had not seen in over 50 years willbe there waiting for him. He parks the car in her driveway, gets out and is instantly greeted by Franco, who is a bundle of energy. Then Conrad sees Mariella. He sees her with his heart pounding in his ears and a big smile on his face as she raced toward him. She is beautiful with the ends of her long silver cardigan flapping in the wind like applause. They embrace for what seemed an eternity…and melt into a kiss that brings back wonderful memories. All the distance, and all the time between them is crushed in the press of his body to hers, his lips to hers.

The days flash and spin. He cooks her waffles. She cooks him soup. They walk her dog, who appears to be not completely offended at the presence of the man. They go to the movies and hold hands in the dark. They laugh and sigh as they flip through the pages of their high school yearbooks. She naps on the couch and, he covers her with a fleece Pittsburgh Steeler blanket. She shows him photo albums from her past. He kisses her fingertips, her palms. He teases her for insisting that the sink stoppers stay in the sink. She teases him for talking about skiing for 35 minutes straight.

Conrad says he has a question for Mariella but first he has to fetch a tissue. He gets up from the couch, goes to his duffle bag and reaches for the velvet box he brought with him.

Returning to the couch he says, "My question is: will you marry me?" And presents her with the white gold, solitaire diamond ring.

Mariella is so taken back she at first does not respond. Conrad asks a second time and she responds with a resounding yes and a big kiss and he puts the ring on her finger. This is a complete surprise to her, unexpected. They are now officially engaged. At night, they close the door against the rest of the world and revel in the kingdom of two they have discovered, more private and wild, more deep and dear, than either had imagined.

She brings him to her church and they pray holding hands. They meet with Father Tim and tell him their story.

"We would like to get married next month," they say.

"You musn't rush things, "he says. *"You mustn't rush grief."* He knows his counsel is useless against their magnetism, but he insists they slow down their breakneck plans. He gives them reading, and they promise to adhere to his advice. They also agree to meet with him again.

She tells him about the best tomatoes for sauce. He tells her about his favorite trip to Italy. They talk about their children and how best to share the news of the wedding. She tells him about Quincy and he shares stories with her about Laura. They weep together for their losses and for the ragged forces of illness and death. She dries his tears with a soft yellow handkerchief and he kisses hers away. The dog helps by nuzzling up to the two of them and by giving them each huge licks.

They agree to share their news with friends so they called Lucinda. They hold one phone, pressing their heads together to hear the congratulations and exclamations. Next they call Paul, and Conrad tells Paul he's met a woman he's going to marry.

There is a slight pause, and Conrad puts Mariella on the line. Paul asks one question. "Did you go to Clementskill High?"

She says, "Yes!"

He responds, "Marilla? I knew it was you."

Mariella takes Conrad to meet two of her closest and dearest friends, Kira and Thomas who had invited them to dinner so they could get to know Conrad. While at their home, Kira counsels Conrad on going to the Episcopal Church the next morning with Mariella. He had never been to any other church and this would be a first for him.

He really appreciates her understanding of his situation and her guidance. Church services the next day are wonderful and inspiring with a 32-member choir. Mariella and Conrad greet Father Tim after the service.

They plan on a wedding in a couple of months figuring Father Tim would give his blessing for a ceremony in June. They'll have plenty of time to send invitations. She strokes his hand and arm. He kisses her forehead silently. They are lovers now. They are a new thing in the universe, a pair of stars borne from the core of something old. They glow.

Chapter 20

Two weeks later, Mariella visited Conrad in New Hampshire just two days after a Nor'easter dumped two feet of new snow. They were together again after what seemed like an eternity, but this time they were in Conrad's house, now warm with companionship and new memories. The happy lovebirds leaned against each other in front of the warm stove.

"I am really tuckered out," yawned Mariella. "How long have I been traveling?"

"Too long," answered Conrad. His eyes were closing of their own will, but his happiness kept jolting him awake with pleased surprise.

"Can you believe the baggage door froze shut?" Mariella laughed, though it hadn't been exactly fun to be stuck at the airport for three hours after her flight had landed at the already late hour of 12:30 a.m.

"Well, the plane didn't want to let you go," Conrad teased. "Which I understand, because neither do I."

He drew her head to his chest, just above his heart, and wrapped his arms around her. "I never want to let you go."

"You are too much," murmured Mariella. "Don't stop."

Outside a light snow settled delicately on top of more than two feet of the newly fallen snow. Conrad couldn't believe the loveliness of it all; it was a delightful scene to welcome Mariella to his New Hampshire home, to their New Hampshire home!

They kissed and nudged and prodded each other until they made it to bed to enjoy a few hours of sleep. Mariella woke once in a start, missing Franco, with a sharp pang in her chest, but then she turned to her love and let the sorrow dissipate against his warmth. She'd see Franco soon enough and soon enough they'd all be together, Conrad and Mariella and Sammy and bright, active Franco, on this unexpected and thrilling adventure.

The next day, weary but filled with energy, the affianced pair tossed their bags into Conrad's trusty car and set off for a three-day vacation in the White Mountains. The time tumbled down as merrily as the snow, with one sweet and tender moment rolling into such laughter and joy that they both felt a little dizzy with good fortune. Luckily, Mariella's common sense prevailed, and they did take moments here and there to catch their breaths.

"Hey there, my Energizer Bunny," Mariella kidded Conrad, "best recharge the batteries so we can go have more fun."

And more fun they had, lacing up ice skates and setting out on the ice as they hadn't done since their teenage years. Their ankles wobbled at first, but soon the old muscle memories from all the times they went skating together in high school kicked in, and they glided, or at least didn't fall, with love and eagerness as their guides.

Later, over a dinner that was as pleasing to look at as it was scrumptious to eat, Mariella set down her fork and reached for Conrad's hand.

"This is so romantic," she said.

"It really is," said Conrad with a soft smile. He squeezed her hand. "It's like something out of a movie."

Mariella laughed. "That's just what my girlfriends at home said! That it was like a fairy tale, or a romance novel."

They drove away from the resort enlivened and giddy. Soon, though, a quieter tone settled over them.

"Are you thinking about dinner tomorrow night?" Conrad took one hand off the wheel and laid it on Mariella's arm.

She nodded. "My first time meeting one of your children. I know they know about me, but they don't know we're engaged. Should we present ourselves as an engaged couple?"

The question lay before them. The last thing they wanted to do, ever, was upset one of their children.

"Maybe not," Conrad offered. "Maybe it would be best if you took the ring off your finger and they can meet you, and then later we can tell them about the engagement."

Mariella held out her hand and admired the ring. "Oh Conrad, it's so beautiful. I still can't believe you proposed on our first night together in North Carolina! It was such a surprise, and you had to ask me a second time as I was at a loss for words."

They shared a delighted, tender glance. "But perhaps you're right. I'll take it off so your children can process the news of us, of me, one step at a time."

The question seemed settled, and they drove home making plans for the future, plans for dinner, plans for the summer and plans for downhill skiing while Mariella was in New Hampshire. When they reached Conrad's house ("*Our* house," he whispered in her ear with a smile), they turned to each other.

"It's strange to hold back information, isn't it?" Mariella said.

Conrad spoke at the same time. "We should let them know now."

Oh, how nervous they were! But how much more they trusted in their love, in their children, and in God to guide them through this uncertain moment. Once they had unpacked, Conrad called his daughter Suzanne and her husband, whom they were to have dinner with the next night, and told them he and Mariella were engaged to be married.

Later, Conrad and Mariella learned Suzanne had called Conrad's older sister to ask what kind of woman Mariella was! Luckily, Aunt Kaye thought the world of Mariella and was happy to tell Suzanne that Mariella was a wonderful person and Suzanne should have no fears for her father. Conrad's daughter Lynne took another tack: she googled 'Mariella' to see what information she could find!

Suzanne was comforted by her aunt's reassurance, but there was still so much to find out about this woman who would soon be a major part of her dad's life. At the following night's dinner, Mariella's natural warmth and charm, and Conrad's obvious happiness, went further to ease any misgivings Suzanne might have had. During the course of the genial and welcoming meal, Mariella mentioned that she and Conrad planned to have a small private wedding with just a few people. Again, she and Conrad didn't want to overwhelm any of the children with elaborate wedding plans.

Suzanne put down her fork. "No way! "If you leave to go to North Carolina I will be leaving an hour later and following you all the way down, and I will camp on the doorstep of the church to be present at my dad's wedding!"

Mariella and Conrad could hardly contain their happiness and gratitude. The next night, they met Conrad's son, Ben, and his wife, and again were met with acceptance and warmth.

"There's always room for one more person in our family, Dad," Ben said, "and we're glad it's Mariella."

At Lynne's house, Conrad and Mariella met more love. "There's no way my dad is going to get married without me being there," said Lynne emphatically.

Mariella's sons also extended their well wishes and congratulations. Her eldest son, Michael, had known since early February his mother had reconnected with her high school sweetheart, and he wished her all the happiness she could want. When she called her younger son, Danny, he had one question for her: "Mom, you aren't going to go to Las Vegas and elope, are you?"

Mariella and Conrad knew now their wedding was going to be a bigger affair with family and friends, but for now they still had the rest of their first time in New Hampshire together to enjoy. They cooked and they walked Sammy, they went out to enjoy the new snow on snowshoes and they snuggled by the warmth of the stove. They drove a few miles to a neighboring ski resort and participated in an afternoon of tubing on the fresh snow. What fun! The following day, Conrad took Mariella to his favorite ski resort where he had a season pass for a day of alpine skiing.

"I love it," Mariella sang as she met Conrad half way down the slope. "I haven't been skiing in 30 years!"

Conrad's heart sang back a happy song that lasted until a little boy who'd lost control of his skis ran into Mariella and knocked her down. Reflecting on the incident later, they referred to him as "the kamikaze kid." Mariella's leg was hurt and bruised, but she now had memories to take back to NC.

Amid all the sweetness and love of this visit, Conrad had another gift to share with his beloved Mariella. For several weeks, he'd been collecting the letters and cards and emails they'd sent to each other, including pictures, notes and a letter from their high school days. He put them all in a three-ring binder and presented it to Mariella.

"Oh, you romantic man!" Tears pricked her eyes, and she laughed at the same time. "I love this. It's right out of a romance novel, all our letters collected like a diary. We're quite the romantics, aren't we?"

He thought his cheeks might break from smiling. "I never thought I was a romantic, but there's something about you that brings it out in me. You are a very special woman, Mariella."

"And you, my knight, are a very special man."

It was hard to let each other go when Mariella had to leave, though they knew that Conrad would be in North Carolina soon and Mariella would be back in New Hampshire. They'd talk and email every day, at least twice a day. It was still hard not to have that hug, that eye contact, all the time. They even missed the inevitable bumps that come when sharing a home with another person, as working through each bump brought them only closer together.

But Mariella did fly home, and Conrad returned to his volunteer work. One day, while helping a young entrepreneur write a marketing plan for his computer repair business, he thought about how pleased Mariella was with the three-ring binder of their letters. *It's like a romance novel,* she'd said. *All my girlfriends say our story is like a fairy tale.*

An idea popped into Conrad's mind. Could their story

actually become a romance novel? He'd never heard of anyone doing that before, but perhaps someone, somewhere, did that sort of thing? Maybe it was a crazy idea, but one could say marrying your high school sweetheart after five decades apart was a crazy idea too. He wasn't going to let that stop him. And imagine, if he could keep it a secret from Mariella, and give the book to her on their wedding day... He smiled to himself. Now that would be romantic!

He realized that the young man was looking at him, waiting for an answer about media saturation, and Conrad quickly put aside his romance novel inspiration. But he couldn't keep a persistent little grin from pulling up one devilish corner of his mouth.

⚉

Thursday, February 28, 5:57 a.m.
From: cholbrook
To: marcuor62
Subject: We are a couple

I will be thinking of you throughout the day today. You will have a wonderful time with your son. Moms know how to love, they just know and you will show it in everything you do.

Soon, soon we will be together again, and soon it will be permanent. I like the sound of that. That is the way it should be. That is the way it was in high school, our friends always saw us together. Took a while, Mariella, but we are finally able to complete the journey we started so many years ago. We were attracted to each other in high school, we enjoyed each other's company, and we shared a lot of personal thoughts and emotions. We were in love with each other and you proudly displayed my high school ring around your neck as the accepted symbol... *We are a couple.*

A few years have passed by, but here we are, and this time there is an engagement ring on your finger to proudly display to others ...*we are a couple*... again!

What a romance novel this would make. I think it is going to end... with the words... *"and they lived happily ever after!"*

Time both flew and crawled as February rolled into March. It was going so fast, yet it couldn't go fast enough until they would be together forever. Conrad spent Easter with Mariella, who put on an enormous Easter dinner spread with delicious food, beautiful Easter decorations, and 14 of her closest friends. When Mariella returned to New Hampshire, she went shopping with Suzanne for a wedding gown and honeymoon clothes. She was successful in purchasing a gorgeous blue gown that Conrad didn't see until their wedding day.

The couple also toured a maple sugaring farm late one evening in March, courtesy of Peter, one of Conrad's neighbors. He showed them how sap was harvested and processed, from tree to evaporator to bottle. Mariella was the guest of honor and got to taste the evening's production, the sweetness almost matching the happiness she felt with her man.

One visit rolled into the next. Conrad and Mariella drove from North Carolina to meet with Elliot and Judy in central North Carolina. Mariella's son George drove up from his home to visit with them. They met two more times with Father Tim.

At the third meeting, Father Tim said they didn't need to meet again. "We were going to meet six times," he said, "but I think you two know what marriage is all about!"

Instead, Conrad and Mariella and Father Tim talked about wedding dates and how the ceremony should run. The couple started wedding planning in earnest, buying wedding bands, ordering invitations, and organizing the reception and pre-wedding gathering. Mariella's organization and Conrad's unflagging energy kept everything running smoothly. They agreed: they could not wait to get married. They couldn't wait to be together all the time.

∞

Monday, April 8, 8:02 a.m.
From: cholbrook
To: marcuor62
Subject: This week

I enjoyed our telephone time last evening and again this morning. You are easy to talk with. It is always a comforting conversation.

We both have a busy day and week ahead of us, and that will help the longing I have for you. Hard to believe our plans are coming together and we will be together this weekend for the rest of our lives.

You are an exciting person to be with, full of love and not afraid to show it. At our age, that is a good thing. We do not need to hold back our feelings about each other. This blessing is unique to us and few people our age get to experience it.

This was meant to happen, the coincidences were indeed too many and putting them together as a whole, I believe this indeed was a miracle and is why God intended for you and I to be left behind in good health so we could complete the love for each other we had so many years ago. Get lots of rest today. You have a lot on your plate to manage. I will be there shortly.

I love you dearly, Mariella,

Conrad

Wednesday, April 10, 12:10 a.m.
From: marcuor62
To: cholbrook
Subject: YOU

Here I am sweetheart... I cannot sleep... I truly need you beside me... Then I am content... I realize after tonight there will four more nights when I am alone and then my entire life changes...

Oh my goodness... I am so excited and also a bit nervous... I am so excited about our new life together, but I am also nervous... I so want to make you happy and please you... I never want to disappoint you or make you sad... I promise to do my very best to make you smile... love you dearly every single minute of every single day...

You will always know how much you mean to me... How deeply I do love you... You truly have been in my dreams for such a very very long time... Now this one dream is coming true... The Lord truly has answered so many of my prayers...

Thank you so much for coming into my life... I have said this before but please remember it... I shall treasure you... the deep love I feel for you is such passion... This has to have developed over the many years...

Conrad... You do make me so very very happy...

Now I am going to try to go back to bed... Solitaire does get old, especially when you win all three kinds of games... Time for some shut eye and wonderful dreams of YOU... I love you dear dear Conrad

Hugs, Mariella

Finally, in the middle of April, Conrad finished the last of his volunteer work. He got in the car with Sammy, drove and drove and drove, and arrived at Mariella's house in North Carolina at 8 a.m. on a Sunday morning to be with his love until time ended. Together, the two went to Sunday services at Mariella's church.

"*Our* church," she whispered to him just before the service began.

Chapter 21

Two nights before the wedding, Mariella and Conrad sat down to a dinner of tacos, which Conrad loved, with Franco hoping beyond all hope they'd get careless with the beans and drop a dollop or two (or more!) on the floor.

It had been a whirlwind since Conrad made the last solo trek from New Hampshire to North Carolina. They'd decided to spend two weeks at their summer home on Hemlock Lake in New England, getting things ready for the season and relaxing together in the beautiful weather. They visited with Mariella's brother-in-law Gerry and his wife, and they spent a wonderful dinner with Mariella's youngest son, Danny.

The wedding was never far from their minds. Indeed, as more and more of their treasured friends told them they planned to come to the ceremony, the more blessed and breathless Conrad and Mariella felt.

Over tacos, a companionable silence fell over the couple. They munched and swallowed, sipped glasses of La Crema, and exchanged small happy smiles. Suddenly, Mariella began to laugh.

Conrad looked at her with concern. "What is it? Did I do something funny? Is everything okay?"

Mariella nodded, trying to get her breath. She settled the laughter, but it bubbled up again in her belly and she couldn't keep it in. Franco started barking along with her laughing. Maybe a walk was in the works for him? Maybe not? Who cared, everyone was making noise!

"Mariella," Conrad felt a smile start to crease his own face, though he had no idea what was making his beloved so giddy. "What in the world is going on?"

She wiped her napkin across her eyes and took a big breath that ended with a last giggle. "My love, everything is wonderful. I'm laughing because I can't believe it's all happening. It's happening! I never thought... Here we are 70-some-odd years young, and happier than we ever thought possible at this stage of our lives. Conrad, we're getting married! In two days, we're getting married."

Mariella rose from her chair and started to dance. She knew she looked silly, but she couldn't help it. Happiness made her buoyant, and music seemed to fill the air. (Plus, if she danced, she wouldn't think about all the vacuuming she ought to do before guests arrived for the pre-wedding get together tomorrow night.)

Conrad watched his bride to be, sway with her arms raised above her head. She was like a flower in bloom, like a Heavenly Blue morning glory opening up to dawn. *We are a couple*! What a miracle this was, both marvelous and strange, because it was so unexpected, as miracles tend to be. *Thank you, Lord,* he whispered. He pushed back his chair and caught up his bride-to-be in his strong arms, and smiled at her with such passion and purity that Mariella felt her knees wobble.

They danced around the kitchen until Franco's barking was a bit too loud to bear, and then petted both dogs with lavish affection.

"Are you nervous?" Conrad wondered if Mariella felt any the butterflies at the thought of so many people coming to celebrate them and their love.

Mariella shook her head. "No," she said. "You'd think I would be, throwing such a big party! But mostly I'm just grateful and sort of shocked, in a nice way, that people want to come be with us on our special day."

Conrad leaned over and kissed her cheek. "I feel the same way. I'm just so excited, I can't wait. There's something I can't wait to — " He cut himself off and got busy scratching behind Sammy's ear.

Mariella looked at him curiously. "You can't wait to what?"

"Oh nothing," Conrad said airily. He'd kept his secret for nearly three months; he wasn't about to blow it. "I just meant I can't wait to get married to the most beautiful, the sexiest, the most loving woman in the world." He kissed her on the lips then, and Mariella forgot what they were talking about.

They returned to the table and started clearing the dishes. "Say," Mariella called out as she ran water over the plates in the kitchen sink. "Did you ever find the three-ring binder with all our letters? I've missed it so much!"

Conrad opened and closed his mouth a few times before turning to take out the garbage to hide his tongue-tied state. "Oh, right," he stuttered. "Yes, Suzanne and Lynne found it at the New Hampshire house when I asked them to look. They'll bring it with them tomorrow. Right, tomorrow." He quickly filled a glass of water and took a long sip.

"Oh good," Mariella said with a happy sigh. "I've missed having those letters with us! Our own little romance novel."

Conrad nearly spat out his water. Coughing, he grabbed a dishcloth and wiped up what he'd spilled.

"I'm fine, I'm fine," he said, as Mariella rushed to his side. "I just can't wait to see those letters, too."

"You old romantic," Mariella teased. "Pretty soon you'll start composing love ballads on a *lute*, for goodness' sake!"

He smiled at her then and gathered her in his arms once again. It was so easy to do that, and it felt so good. "For you, my love, I'll write poems in the sky."

They kissed each other, and both forgot the conversation, the dishes, the dogs, the people coming tomorrow night, the ceremony the day after that to bind their love before God.

When you're very lucky, sometimes all that exists is a kiss.

Ninety-nine people were invited to the wedding, and more than 60 of them came to Mariella and Conrad's house for an informal get-together with pizza, beer and wine.

Mariella glowed with beauty, Conrad with eager energy. Friends of one met the other, and everyone noted how happy the two made each other.

One by one, Mariella's best girlfriends pressed Mariella into loving hugs. "You look amazing," Lucinda whispered.

"I couldn't be happier for you," MaryJo said with a happy sniffle.

Elliot and Judy mingled with the crowd as proud and happy as parents at their child's wedding. They approved mightily of Conrad and extracted promises from the couple to visit them as often as possible.

"You've always got a home with us," Elliot said to them. "But you have a home with each other now, and it's just wonderful to see."

He turned to Conrad with a mock-glower and a wink. "Treat her wrong, though, buddy, and watch out!"

"Don't worry, Elliot," Conrad said. "It's my job to make sure Mariella is happy for the rest of her life. I am going to take that job very, very seriously!"

On and on it went, this joyous tribe celebrating the imminent union of two such kind, hardworking, Christian souls. Guests lingered long after the last pizza box was empty. No one wanted to leave the circle of Conrad and Mariella's love, but finally Suzanne and Lynne shepherded the last guests away, claiming that the bride and groom needed to rest. Then they left, and Conrad and Mariella sat down in the living room.

"Tomorrow, darling," murmured Mariella.

"Tomorrow, my love," Conrad whispered back. All the lovers in the world had never known such perfect bliss, a feeling that electrified them and calmed them at the same time.

"Thank goodness we're old," said Mariella.

"What do you mean?" Conrad was puzzled.

"If we were young, I don't think we could handle this much unexpected happiness. We'd get scared or dissatisfied, thinking that maybe there was something better around the bend. Teenagers are trying on new lives all the time. We've been around the block. We can accept a blessing and multiply it by a million with our love," Mariella said.

Conrad stroked her hair. "My philosopher! Maybe you're right. We had to reach this point in our lives to be ready for each other."

"Is your suit ready?" Mariella leaned against his chest.

"Yes. Is your gown ready?"

"Yes."

"Did you write your vows?"

"Yes. Did you?"

"Of course."

They sat in silence. "So I guess we're ready," Conrad said.

"I guess we are," said Mariella. "This is the first time in my life that I have faith that everything is going to come together. I feel downright relaxed!"

"Hey Mariella?"

"Yes, Conrad?"

"Want to get married tomorrow?"

She closed her eyes and smiled. "Yes, Conrad. I do."

The tears started flowing even before Mariella and Conrad, both resplendent in their wedding attire, Mariella's blue gown causing more than a few murmurs of approving awe, entered All Souls Episcopal Church. Every pew was filled with family and friends, many of whom were more used to attending funerals these days rather than weddings.

It was as if the friendly ghosts of all the weddings previous were hovering in the air above Mariella and Conrad, blessing them with generations of love-memories.

The whole place was all like a song, a chorus whose harmonies rang long and slow, with such humble richness, that the tears felt cleansing, like they came from a deep, pure place to which they all belonged, no matter the trials or failures they faced. The greatest of all these was love, and Conrad and Mariella shared with their friends and family the gift they had been given.

They couldn't believe who had decided to make the trek to North Carolina for the wedding — nintey-nine people from fifteen states, Mariella's siblings and all of Conrad's siblings. Quincy's brother and his wife came with all of their children, and one of their grandchildren with his fiancée and three step-children insisted that they wanted to be part of the celebration—that's how much they loved Mariella and had come to love Conrad.

Quincy's closest cousin and her husband were in the crowd, having told Mariella that they knew how well she took care of Quincy, and that they loved her as much as Quincy. Conrad's cousin, Hank, came from Wisconsin, and he remembered meeting Mariella in 1958 at a Christmas dance when he visited Conrad in Clementskill

Father Tim welcomed all to the ceremony with grace and such generosity of spirit that the attendees immediately felt comfortable in the lovely church, which had been built in the early 1900s by George Vanderbilt for his daughter's wedding. A spirit of love and family togetherness permeated the entire room.

When the religious part of the ceremony was over, everyone moved into a reception hall where Mariella and

Conrad would cut the cake. Hugs and kisses and laughter filled the room. Mariella slipped her shoes off once the formal pictures were taken and spent the rest of the time barefoot at their reception. Conrad's children and Mariella's children congratulated them for how beautiful they looked and how happy they clearly were. Soon, the newly married couple moved to the front of the room to exchange the vows they had written to each other.

Mariella went first.

"Conrad," she said, "you complete me as a person. You are the missing piece in my heart, my mind, my soul, my body, my life. Your love, warmth, and tenderness give me a feeling of total happiness beyond words. I am yours forever until God calls one of us to his heavenly kingdom. I will be at your side through whatever challenges are ahead for us. We will laugh, love, and cry together. You are my rock, my mighty oak, my sweetheart, my best friend, my confidant, my security blanket, my Energizer bunny, my handsome prince — my love! I love you,

I respect you, I trust you, I adore you. I am yours,
you are mine forever..."

Women dabbed at their eyes with handkerchiefs. Couples wound their arms around each other's waists. Young people hoped they too would know such love when they reached their senior years. Then Conrad began to speak.

"Margo, you are my treasure. You captured my heart 56 years ago and you have done it again. Today we have committed to each other in God's house with his blessing, our marriage to each other. I am so appreciative that you love me. I will not disappoint you. You my dear are the joy of my life now. I love you, Mariella. Many years ago, my lips revealed those words for the first time. On January 1 this year, I once again committed myself to you using those words. Today we have cemented these words with our marriage. You will hear them daily from me for the rest of our time on our Lord's beautiful Earth and they will also be the last words you hear coming from my lips. I love you so much, I could write a book....... In fact, I have!"

Mariella beamed at him. Her heart was so full she didn't entirely hear what he was saying, but she knew that no soul had ever felt the love and gratitude she did for her husband, her *husband!* Conrad was her *husband!* It was as if she were floating on clouds of prayer and joy. She realized he was still talking, and their friends and family looked especially awed, so she tuned back into his words.

"Back in early March, I gave our three-ring binder of close to 300 letters to a professional writer and commissioned her to write a full-length romance novel about our lives and our relationship. Suzanne was the editor, and I believe she has something for the two of us..."

He stepped back, beaming, as his daughter walked to the front of the room. He looked at Mariella, and by the stunned look on her face, he knew that while she heard the words, she couldn't fully grasp the admittedly far-out possibility that there was reality to them. Suzanne also saw that Mariella wasn't fully aware of what was being presented to her, and first, with great gentleness, gave her the three-ring binder filled with the letters and cards and photographs.

Later, Mariella told Conrad that this was the "book" she thought he was talking about, and when Suzanne reached into a bag and pulled out yet another book, she had no idea what was happening. It was an oversized hardback. She opened the cover and revealed inside it another, smaller book with a photo of two young people walking up a hill holding hands. Suzanne held up the novel, titled "Always in My Heart," and opened it to the dedication page. She read it aloud to the awe struck utterly impressed guests.

This book is dedicated to the memory of Quincy Sellesbury and Laura Holbrook, beloved spouses of Mariella and Conrad. We talk about them frequently with thoughts of wonderful and enjoyable times spent over the years. Quincy and Laura loved us deeply, as we did them and they were dedicated to making us happy. We believe Laura and Quincy would be pleased with the happiness Mariella and Conrad have found with each other and will be sharing for the remainder of our lives.

Everyone gasped and exclaimed. It was the most romantic, extravagant gesture anyone could imagine. To think that Conrad had thought of such a rare, expansive and special expression of his love for Mariella and the beauty of their love story, and had managed to keep such a big project a secret for three months — well, the women had wobbly knees and the men couldn't believe what they now had to live up to!

Conrad looked across the room and caught the eye of Paul, his high school best friend and his best man today, for the second time in his life. Paul nodded, grinned, and gave him a thumbs-up Conrad would remember for the rest of his life.

But the best reaction was from Mariella, his blue-gowned love. Suzanne handed her the book, and she took it with eyes as wide as dinner plates. Her heart was beating so fast she may as well have run a marathon. Conrad had done this for her, for *her*. She turned and wrapped her arms around his neck as hard as she could. She still couldn't believe what was happening, but she'd felt the book in her hands. She'd put on her glasses to skim the flyleaf, though she hadn't been able to absorb more than a word or two. It was real, all of this was real.

She felt like she could fly. She knew if she did, if magically all the happiness in her heart gave her wings, that Conrad would be right next to her holding her hand, zooming up to the sky.

Chapter 22

The next morning, Mariella and Conrad woke at 4 a.m.

The reception had been a dizzy delight, with cake and dancing and chatting. Mariella's boys looked handsome, so much like Quincy it amazed her, and she was prouder than she could say to have them by her side. Conrad's daughters were utterly beautiful and his son so handsome, and their respective husbands and wives a joy to behold. Everyone told Conrad and Mariella that this was one of the sweetest, most meaningful weddings they had ever been to. It was the way weddings should be.

Amazingly, the newlyweds weren't tired in the slightest when they woke. Rather, they were bright, alert and simply thrilled to be married.

"Conrad," said Mariella, brushing her hair. "Why don't we head out on our honeymoon right now? We've got a long drive ahead of us, so why wait? I'm chipper as anything, and I'll bet my Energizer bunny is too."

Conrad gave her a big grin. "I think that's a great idea, my wife."

They hugged. "I'm glad you think so, my husband," Mariella said with a kiss.

They gathered their things, and Conrad checked them out of the hotel where they'd stayed, rather than drive all the way back to the house. He packed up the car with his customary thoroughness, and Mariella found some snacks for them to munch as they drove.

Elliot and Judy had suggested that they honeymoon on Ocrakoke Island on the Outer Banks of North Carolina — and what a marvelous idea it was. Conrad and Mariella made the eight-hour drive in time to catch an early ferry, on which they met some delightful fellow travelers.

Everything seemed tinged with grace, from the ferry ride to the B&B suite that they'd reserved in advance. Not only did they have a 360-degree view of the bay and the charming little town, but they had their very own "widow's walk." Mariella was just glad they were both in good shape, as their suite was four flights up!

In gorgeous weather, husband and wife walked barefoot on the beautiful white sand beaches, went out to dinner, and met the most genial and convivial folks at the B&B breakfasts.

They shared their story and basked in the good feeling it seemed to evoke in everyone. They soaked up other people's stories. They reveled in the other's happiness and gave thankful prayers for the blessing of each other.

On their last morning, a guest at breakfast asked them what they planned to do next, now that they were married.

Conrad and Mariella looked at each other. Conrad spoke first.

"Well, we plan to go to our summer home In New England," he said. "And we'll spend time at our home in New Hampshire, and visit our children and grandkids as much as possible."

"That's for sure," said Mariella with an emphatic nod. "As happy as we are, there's nothing like family. It's the most important thing. I have three gorgeous granddaughters, and I cannot wait to see them. Conrad's family is just amazing and so kind, and my sons are truly always in my heart."

Conrad squeezed her hand. How he loved this passionate woman, who spoke about emotions with such skill and warmth.

Mariella squeezed back. How she loved this passionate man, who made the world bigger and more beautiful with his energy and mind.

The guest brushed tears away from her eyes. "You two are pretty special, but I think a lot of people must tell you that, right? Anyway, I'm curious, where do you see yourselves down the line? You know, ten, fifteen years from now?"

Mariella laughed. "We already have our 21st wedding anniversary planned! We'll sit on the front porch and get our rocking chairs going in the same rhythm so we can kiss," she said.

The guest sighed. "It's just like the ending to a romance novel," she said.

"Yes," Conrad and Mariella said at the same time with huge smiles on their beautiful faces, their hearts joined across memories and time. "Yes, it really is."

And they lived happily ever after...

All proceeds from this book are being donated to "Children First" a nonprofit organization headquartered in Asheville, NC and also to the music program of All Souls Cathedral in Biltmore Village, Asheville, NC.